# deerstalker

# DEER STALKER

## NICOLE M. ZAUNBRECHER

*Deerstalker*

© 2025 by Nicole M. Zaunbrecher

Editors: Deborah Froese, Joshua Owens, Noëlla Simmons
Cover and Interior Design: Emma Elzinga

Indigo River Publishing
3 West Garden Street, Ste. 718
Pensacola, FL 32502
www.indigoriverpublishing.com

Ordering Information:

Quantity Sales: Special discounts are available on quantity purchases by corporations, associations, and others. For details, contact the publisher at the address above.

Orders by US trade bookstores and wholesalers: Please contact the publisher at the address above.

Printed in the United States of America

Library of Congress Control Number: 2024918983
ISBN: 978-1-964686-17-2 (paperback)   978-1-964686-18-9 (ebook)
First Edition

With Indigo River Publishing, you can always expect great books, strong voices, and meaningful messages. Most importantly, you'll always find . . . *words worth reading.*

*For my mother,*
*who encouraged me to publish this book and couldn't wait to read it.*

# Acknowledgements

I would like to thank the many writer's groups who helped to shape this story into a novel, including: Theresa Marie Kenney of Duss, Kenney, Safer, Hampton & Joos, P.A., for giving us a space to workshop; John Boles, for leading our group and providing outstanding editing services; Sharron Finch, for inviting me to this wonderful group and chatting about our stories for hours afterward; Marcella Ann Beeching, for providing feedback; Holly and Jaylan Phoenix, for encouragement; Janet D'Andrea, for inspiration; and Thomas Cumiskey, for the cutest section titles I have ever seen.

This book would not be possible without the encouragement and support of my family, namely Dwayne Zaunbrecher, Shari Kirkenmeier, and Sandra Kirkenmeier; my biggest and loudest cheering squad. They wanted me to pursue my dreams of becoming an author.

Organizations like NaNoWriMo gave me the time and space to write, and literary conferences like the Florida Heritage Book Festival gave me insight into the life of an author; as well as allowed me to make new friends.

And of course, I would like to thank the publisher, Indigo River Publishing, for taking a chance on me, and my editors, who polished the rock I gave them into a diamond.

## "The Road Not Taken"

Two roads diverged in a yellow wood,
And sorry I could not travel both
And be one traveler, long I stood
And looked down one as far as I could
To where it bent in the undergrowth;

Then took the other, as just as fair,
And having perhaps the better claim,
Because it was grassy and wanted wear;
Though as for that the passing there
Had worn them really about the same,

And both that morning equally lay
In leaves no step had trodden black.
Oh, I kept the first for another day!
Yet knowing how way leads on to way,
I doubted if I should ever come back.

I shall be telling this with a sigh
Somewhere ages and ages hence:
Two roads diverged in a wood, and I—
I took the one less traveled by,
And that has made all the difference.

## – ROBERT FROST

# Table of Contents

# Prologue

## WANING CRESCENT MOON

## 1635

**H**is lungs filled with crisp air that blew hot out of his nose. His feet pounded into the ground, the only sound in the forest louder than his heartbeat. The trees were dark, with scatters of moonbeams penetrating through the tops. Low-hanging branches brushed against mangled skin as he ran forward. All around him was death and decay. He reveled in it. The taste of ash and dust was on his tongue, a flavor he knew all too well. Coming upon his prey, he lunged forward without warning. A short shriek pierced the quiet night. Blood dripped from his maw, sizzled and hit the dirt, mingling with the taste of ever-present death. Sated, he left the rest of the corpse to rot along with the foliage and trees surrounding it.

Wendell's eyes flew open to reveal the oaken beams of the ceiling, dark amidst the shadows created by the light emanating from a near-by window. His heart slammed against his ribcage, his breath ragged. Dirt and sweat caked his taut, sore limbs. The blurry trees and bushes were still flashing in his mind and the strong fragrance of fir mixed with the scent of ever-present death lingering in the air.

"Wendell, breakfast is ready!" a voice called.

Wendell sat up, taking deep breaths until the raggedness receded into an even pace. Instead of the dark forest, he was in his room. The worn wooden walls were a familiar enough sight to make him sigh with relief. He got out of the old rickety bed—his father's, when he was a boy—and splashed his face, running his hands through blond hair that stopped just at his chin. Wendell glanced at his reflection in the ripples of the water, large dark eyes with oblong pupils stared back at him. Above the washbasin was a print with drawings of the moon phases and their names, sketched by a visiting scholar when he was younger. Wendell stared at the drawing of a new moon, black and empty, before taking a deep breath. He then washed his arms and legs with cold water from a bucket on the floor, then pulled on a gray linen tunic and brown lederhosen. The rest of his room was sparse, made up of a light brown dresser given to the family many years ago and a cuckoo clock his grandfather made to commemorate his birth. The clock was intricately carved, with the shape of trees made of dark wood symbolizing the forest surrounding their village and three pinecones hanging from the bottom. Bears, deer, squirrels, and other woodland creatures intermingled with the trees.

Wendell stepped out into the dark hallway, feeling the worn timber beneath his bare feet. The walls held a few small oval portraits of his family—though none featured him. The savory scent of pork hung heavy in the air, growing stronger as Wendell approached the dining area. A simple oak table in the middle of the room was large enough to seat six, but only four chairs were set out.

"Good morning, Grandfather," Wendell greeted the old man tending to the morning's meal.

"Good morning, Wendell. Did you sleep well?" his grandfather replied.

"Yes, Grandfather," he lied. His parents were already sitting down across from each other, stoneware plates and bowls set in front of each seat. They did not acknowledge him as he entered the room and sat down at the far end of the table, waiting for breakfast to be served. His parents were stiff, the outlines of their bones peeking out from beneath their linen clothing. His mother's eyes were sunken and dark. A large plate was placed in the center of the table, steam rising from the freshly cooked bratwurst. Figs and berries complemented the sausage. His grandfather sat at the other end of the table, facing Wendell. They each took pieces for their own plate. Wendell reached further across the empty space where two more people could fit on either side. Noticing Wendell's outstretched arm attempting to grab a piece of bread, his grandfather pushed the serving plate closer toward him.

"Let us pray," Wendell's grandfather said once everyone had their food. They all clasped hands. "Lord, thank you for blessing us with this food which we are about to eat. Please keep us under your protection. Amen."

"Amen," the family murmured. Their cutlery clinked against the plates as they ate.

"Have you heard news of the war, Hansel?" the old man asked, eyeing his son-in-law with interest.

Hansel, a middling man with rough skin and hands from working on a farm, glanced up from his meal. "We've been discussing it all week," he replied. "It's not likely to end any time soon." He shook his head. "I find it hard to believe that all of this bloodshed is God's Will."

"And what of the bloodshed here each month?" Wendall's mother asked, staring at her plate.

Wendell stopped eating, his stomach twisting.

The old man slammed his fist down on the table in shock. "Marla!"

"What, Father?" Marla raised her voice, gazing fiercely at him. "We all know what happens!" Her hands clenched the fork and knife tightly, face contorting into a grimace of rage.

Hansel laid a hand on his wife's arm before briefly glancing at his son. His eyes showed no love or pity, only an acknowledgment of Wendell's existence. The room was quiet and tense. Eventually, Marla started to eat again.

Wendell's chair scraped against the floor as he stood and gave a small bow. "Thank you for the meal, Grandfather." He could not stomach another bite as bile rose to his throat, the burning sensation leaving a sour taste on the back of his tongue. He caught his grandfather's gaze. The old man nodded wearily, smiling at him.

"Where are you going?" his mother asked with a cold-eyed glare.

"To the Hall," Wendell told her without meeting her gaze. Anywhere was better than being there, with their judgment and loathing tainting the very air he breathed. He rushed out of the house to escape the animosity inside. When he was younger, he cried, but at twenty he was used to the loneliness and derision. It didn't make it any easier, though.

As he walked down the familiar dirt path to the town hall with his head down, doors and windows noisily slammed shut on the old homes he passed. He turned the corner and noticed a small group of people conversing by the baker's shop.

". . . the poor thing is so gaunt," a woman was saying in a hushed voice.

"No wonder, having a son like that would make me lose my appetite as well," a man said brusquely, his arms crossing over his chest.

They stopped talking abruptly as soon as they spotted his approach and glared at him before dispersing in different directions. Wendell's sharp hearing picked up a mumbled "monster" as one of the men walked away.

The path became quiet and deserted, with only him to wander down it.

The town hall came into sight soon, a large pale building that served as a meeting place, knowledge center, and entertainment venue for the whole village. It was scarcely used these days, which was why he ventured there often. It smelled a bit musty most times, but Wendell didn't mind. The wooden floors lightly creaked from his footsteps as he made his way to the back corner to browse the dusty library shelves. Scrolls, leatherbound tomes, and books in various states of use were crowded together based on author and topic. Journals of scientific import to the medical community contained diagrams and drawings Wendell couldn't quite comprehend. The philosophies of Aristotle and the star charts of Galileo fascinated him. But what brought him here often were the printed tales originally passed down through oral tradition.

Wendell would usually tuck himself away into a dimly lit corner and read adventure books that were brought in by the travelers who came into town to stay for the night. Stories from all over the world, across the vast seas and rolling plains, were held within the walls of his personal refuge. A man, who appeared to be a scholar from his stately clothes, was nearby thumbing through some of the advanced medical texts on a higher shelf. He paid Wendell no heed, walking past without a sideways glance.

Wendell pulled out a tattered scroll from one shelf and made his way to a familiar dark plush chair. As he read the scroll, his head tilted down until his chin nearly touched his chest and his bangs fell into his eyes. He tucked the loose strands behind his ear. Being alone in this space was more comfortable than feeling alone in his own home despite the presence of his family. It was warm and quiet there in a way that made his tense muscles relax and his breathing even out as he focused on the faraway journeys of travelers. He did not have to tune out harsh arguments or avoid stinging glares from those who were supposed to love and care for him. Here, he could spend the day enveloped in an imaginary world where he wasn't so different from everyone else.

# 1

# The Lone Traveler

**Jacques followed a narrow path** within a dense forest, brown and gold leaves crunching beneath his boots. The air was crisp and fresh, smelling like dewy bark. His haggard breathing was loud around him, disrupted only by a skittering among the brush or the calls of a bird. It was cold out. The sweat drying on his skin felt like ice and the hair on his arms stood up.

When the traveler got to a crossroads, he pulled out an old, crumpled map from the sack slung around his shoulder and peered at it closely, trying to find the area he was in. "Have I gone far enough?" he murmured to himself. With a shrug, he tucked the map back into his bag and continued down the left fork. His clothes were stiff and dirty from being washed in streams, his legs tight and sore from endless walking and hiking, and his stomach ached in want of food.

The trail grew smaller and the woods turned darker. Trees enclosed all around him, blocking the sunlight from hitting the hard ground below. In the dimness, he saw piles of branches and thick tree limbs stacked upon each other for a great distance around. Red pieces of cloth were tied on several of them, fluttering in the cool breeze. A narrow path broke through the encasement. Slowing down, he wondered if he should continue.

Something in the air tugged at him, a smell that was all too familiar on the wind. *Food, there's food up ahead!* Jacques gasped and rushed forward, swatting at low-hanging leaves as twigs scratched his face. Before he knew it, he stumbled upon a village.

And quite the village it was. Just as fast as he arrived, the traveler came to a halt with his mouth slightly open, eyes taking in the scene before him. The old and worn buildings had lasted through several generations—yet he noted the patchwork roofing and inconsistent colorations of the walls, indicating that life was still being breathed into them. The dirt road leading into the center of town had divots from the wheels of carriages and carts, the packed earth showing signs of hoofprints in dried mud and specks of grass. A few rocks were embedded in the ground, having been churned up from beneath the earth. The air seemed muted compared to other places he had traveled through. It was quiet in a way that had him on edge, although he could not quite discern why.

As he wandered down the empty dirt pathway, he marveled at the oddities of his surroundings. Strings of rope and leather with bits of odds and ends tied on were hanging from the rooftops and near doorways of several buildings. Strange carved statues of half-human, half-animal creatures stood at the front of most structures he could see.

"Where is everyone?" he said aloud, frowning. It was too quiet, making him nervous. The village was abandoned despite the smell of freshly baked bread coming from deeper within.

His eyes darted around in search of any townspeople. Instead, they kept focusing on the hanging strings. He took a few steps closer to examine a pair at the nearest edifice. One leather cord had sharp pointed teeth, claws, and gray-brown fur woven into it. Scrunching up his face, he tried to determine which animals the artifacts were from and why they were strung up in the middle of an eerie hamlet. Out of the corner of his eye, he saw someone walk by and pause near him.

Turning toward the villager, Jacques was startled at the sight of a meat cleaver dripping with fresh blood in the man's hand. His heart thudded inside of his chest, breath picking up as he watched the bright red liquid slide down the blade and splatter onto the ground. Pieces of meat clung to the blade's edge, the smell sharp and tangy.

"How did you manage to find your way to this place?" the villager asked in a deep baritone, face scrunched up. He appeared to be as startled to see Jacques as the traveler was of seeing the bloody cleaver.

Jacques winced and rubbed the back of his head, glancing away. "I suppose I got a little lost," he said.

"You should not linger here long, stranger," the man with the cleaver replied. From the dirty apron wrapped around his bulky form, Jacques guessed he was a butcher.

An eerie feeling made the hair at the back of Jacques' neck stand up. From the butcher's earlier reaction at his arrival, Jacques assumed this village didn't receive many visitors. If that was the case, why did the man try to scare him away? He glanced back down at the knife and swallowed thickly before replying, "My name is Jacques," feeling opposed to being called a stranger in this strange place. "These parts aren't on the map I have. Is there a map maker here?"

The butcher pointed with his tool in the direction of a few more buildings. "The cartographer from the city is set up in town. Second building to the left. Best be on your way."

Jacques thought better of asking the butcher about the dangling charms and instead hurried in the direction he was pointing to. "Thank you!" he called over his shoulder. The villager was still staring at him, mouth set in a thin line.

As he made his way to the mapmaker at the end of the road, Jacques realized why the village seemed so eerie when he first stumbled upon it. Even the forest around him had the same feeling of stillness and trepidation. No birds chirped or cawed to each other, no small animals rustled within the brush or jumped between trees. The appearance of the structures had struck him so suddenly because no other signs of life brimmed within the area. He frowned, hiking his bag up farther onto his shoulder. Perhaps it was the silence of early winter when most animals would turn to hibernation to escape the cold.

Jacques entered the shop. It smelled a bit moldy, but he felt at ease when he saw the maps, compasses, and travelers' wares spread about shelves and tables. A wiry man with long, thin gray hair stood with his back to the door, leaning over a desk lit by a single lamp. As Jacques neared, he saw the man drawing a new map.

"Oh, I've yet to see a mapmaker at work; mind if I watch?" he asked excitedly.

The cartographer twitched, his pen slurring across the page at the movement. He let out a sound of disappointment and eyed Jacques over his shoulder through his round glasses. "Look what you've done now," he said in a gruff, weary voice.

Jacques leaned back, hands coming up in front of him. "My apologies, sir! I did not intend on startling you. Please, can it be fixed?"

The mapmaker faced him fully. "You cannot erase what has been done; the ink will smudge." He squinted at Jacques, just like the butcher had. "What is it you seek, traveler?"

"Well, I," Jacques began, glancing at the ruined map behind the man. "I need a new map to find my way."

The cartographer nodded and walked away from his unfinished work toward shelves lined with bound sheets of paper. "What kind of map?"

Jacques took a breath, his shoulders letting go of some tension. "Well, the one I have doesn't show the roads around here, just the forest. I'd like to see what else is in this area."

The older man reached an arm behind him, palm up. Jacques blinked. "Well give me the one you have, then," the cartographer said sharply.

Jacques quickly placed his crumpled, dirtied map in the man's hand and watched as it was examined. After a moment, the mapmaker started pulling some of the wrapped papers off the shelves.

"Where are you headed? South? You're far from the sea here, though I have oceanic drawings. Or if mountains you seek, I have northern guides."

"Nowhere in particular as of yet," Jacques answered, fingers curling and uncurling around the strap of his bag.

The cartographer glanced at him down the bridge of his slender nose over small circular glasses. His long shaggy hair hung forward, framing his face. "What brings you out here, with no destination in mind?"

Jacques paused with his fidgeting, the question catching him off guard. After a moment, he said, "Just wanted to travel, is all. Explore the world while I can."

The man swept his gaze up and down the traveler. "Mmhmm." He put a few of the maps back and then handed Jacques the rest. "Try these, you may find them useful for this area."

Jacques nodded, unraveling the bindings on the top one. Opening it up, he saw the usual markings and lines of his own map—but instead of wilderness, the village was drawn out in detail at the center of the woods. "Sorry, what do these indicate?" he asked, pointing to a few symbols around the village.

The cartographer shuffled through some papers as he replied. "Landmarks of sorts. Mostly for those who live nearby or frequently travel through the area."

Jacques nodded again, still staring at the markings. They were like the hanging totems and statues he saw outside: one mark appeared to be a long tooth, the other a hoof, and the third antlers. "So, are these the kinds of animals in the area, then?"

The man glanced at Jacques, averting his eyes quickly,

and hummed.

"I'll take it, what is the price?"

The map maker pointed at the amount scribbled in one of the corners.

Jacques lowered the map. "Ah . . . I don't have that much."

The cartographer put his hands behind his back in a contemplative pose, his thin, white beard coming to his chest. "What do you have to trade?"

Jacques set the map down and rummaged through his rucksack. It didn't hold much, just a few pairs of worn pants and tunics, wooden cups he used for water and food, and a tool to mark distance that he was still figuring out how to use properly. A few other items clanked around as he dug the device out, thinking it was probably the most valuable and useful. He held it up for the cartographer to examine.

The man simply pointed to a shelf housing the same tool, though less dirty and more advanced.

"Oh," Jacques put the tool back in his bag.

"No destination to your journey, no money or items to trade, no sense of where you are..." the cartographer mumbled, squinting at him again and peering closer. "What are you running away from?"

# 2

# The Fated Meeting

**Wendell wasn't quite sure when** he started to notice it, but a buzzing in his ears—the footsteps and hushed voices—finally caught his attention. He stopped reading the record he was halfway through to see a group of townspeople huddled close together, whispering frantically. Their eyes occasionally darted over to him. He didn't hear his name, nor any of the slurs they usually called him when they thought he couldn't hear them, but their topic was still interesting to him. Something about the urgency in their voices sped up his heartbeat.

"A traveler arrived this morning," one villager whispered. "He looks young. I saw him talking with Fleischer and then he was running out of the mapmaker's setup."

"Yes, he bumped into my cart, made me spill half the contents," another grumbled.

"What shall we do about him?" a third asked.

"We'll do what we always do—tell him to leave before it's too late."

The conversation stopped and the group cast stinging glares at

Wendell. Hunching lower in his seat, he brought the scroll up to disappear behind the parchment. *No,* he thought. *The newcomer can leave the village without knowing of my presence.*

The townspeople dispersed after a moment. No doubt the entire community would know about the troublesome stranger soon enough.

By now the memories of his abuse during childhood were as cold as the ice on top of the Alps, but the scars were still there, as a reminder. Wendell learned to fold himself into the shadows, staying silent, to avoid the ire of his neighbors. The town hall was the only place still open to him, by the grace of his grandfather's protests that he needed an education.

Wendell stayed until the candles were burning low and an elder finally approached him with a nervous, yet firm, facial expression. He set the records he had been reading aside, almost finished with them, and begrudgingly started on his way home.

Walking with his head down, he watched his feet so as not to trip over loose twigs and stones. *I missed dinner again.* His arms were wrapped around him to ward off the chill of the cold night air.

Jacques shuffled his feet on the dirt road, hands stuffed into his pockets. He shivered as the wind picked up. He had left the mapmaker's shop in a hurry after stammering out a response to the man's question. Not paying attention to where he was going, he ended up bumping into a villager's cart. After apologizing profusely and attempting to put the items back in the cart, he found himself searching for a place to stay for the night.

"Have you some coin?" the innkeeper asked.

Jacques sighed, shaking his head. "Perhaps a trade?" he offered hopefully.

The gruff man frowned at him. "We don't barter for beds here."

Jacques dipped his head and wandered around the village as the sun dipped low in the sky.

"Suppose I should just leave," he muttered to himself. The idea of making camp in the woods did not appeal to him, as he longed for a soft, warm bed to lie on. He glanced up and caught sight of someone along the path in front of him. Hope brimming in his chest for a moment, he called out, "Hello there!"

The person halted and Jacques jogged closer to a young man about a foot shorter than him. "Sorry for yelling out," he said, out of breath. "But no one else is around, and I need help."

The other stared at him, unblinking. "What kind of help?" he asked.

"I'm tired and hungry, is there someplace I can stay for the night?"

He pointed to a building at the end of the road. "There's the inn."

Jacques noted the direction he was pointing and sighed, rubbing his neck. "I have no coins or items to trade."

"Oh."

They stood in the center of the dirt road for a moment. The air was cold and still around them.

"Is there anywhere—" Jacques began.

"I'm sorry—" the young man said at the same time.

Jacques smiled and gestured to him. "Please, after you."

The other shook his head. "I would not advise you to stay the night here. It is not safe."

"Ah," Jacques said, ducking his head. "You are not the first person to say that today. Seems like everyone in this village wants me gone."

The young man finally blinked, mouth forming an *o*, but no words came out. Jacques abruptly murmured his gratitude for the help and began to walk away.

"Young traveler, need you a place to rest for the night?" an older man's voice called out into the night.

Jacques stopped, whirling around to the source of the voice. "Yes!"

he said in a hopeful, desperate tone.

"You may stay the night with us," an old man told him. He was standing on the porch of a home close by.

"Grandfather!" the young man exclaimed. Jacques wasn't sure what to make of the shock in his voice.

"Are you sure?" He glanced from one to the other. "I would rather like not to cause trouble, as I have already stirred things up enough as it is."

"Ah, so you were the one causing a ruckus earlier!" the elder accused, hands on his hips.

"N-no . . . well, yes, sir, I suppose," Jacques stammered out, wringing his hands. He took a breath. "I apologize, I didn't mean anything by it."

The older man broke out into a hearty laugh. "I'm only teasing. Come in out of the cold."

Jacques grinned and mounted the steps. "Thank you very much, sir."

"The name is Albrecht," the man replied. "And yours?"

"Jacques."

"So where are you from, Jacques?" Albrecht asked as they walked inside. The grandson followed behind silently.

"Lorraine," Jacques replied.

"Ah," Albrecht said, eyebrows raised. He nodded, then turned to his grandson. "I shall inform your parents."

As they waited for Albrecht to return, Jacques turned and asked, "Pardon me, I forgot to introduce myself and here I am in your home. I'm Jacques." He gave a small smile and offered his hand.

The other hesitated for a moment. "Wendell," he finally replied, giving Jacques' hand a small shake. Then he quickly turned his head in his grandfather's direction. Jacques strained to pick up any sounds but heard nothing.

"Excuse me," Wendell murmured and headed down the hallway,

disappearing around a corner.

"Why have you brought the traveler here? Do you want him to die in our own house?" his mother hissed as Wendell approached. He stood out of sight, listening in.

"Marla, the new moon is still a day away. He's just passing through," his grandfather replied sternly.

"Then who will be the sacrifice this time?" she asked in a thin voice.

"Would you have him sleep out in the woods?" his grandfather asked, appalled. "I did not raise you to forgo compassion for weary travelers. Have you forgotten where our family came from? How we got here?"

Marla averted her gaze, biting her lip and crossing her arms over her chest.

"Albrecht, you know how dangerous this is," Wendell's father told him, his voice low.

"He has nowhere else to go, and someone has to show him kindness in this godforsaken village," the old man spat. He sighed after a moment, rubbing his forehead. "I apologize, my dear boy. That was rude of me."

Wendell stared down at his feet, already dreading having to tell the weary traveler that he could not stay with them.

His father pursed his lips, placing his hands on his hips. "We can allow him to stay the night," he began. Wendell's head shot, mouth opening slightly in shock. "But if he is not gone by tomorrow, his blood will be spilled," he added sharply, jaw clenching. With that, he whirled around and ushered Wendell's mother back into their room.

Wendell's grandfather let out a weary, long exhale. After a moment, he turned the corner to give Wendell a curt nod. They both walked back down the hall.

"You are welcome to rest here for tonight, but I suggest you head out in the morning," Albrecht said as the two returned to the foyer where Jacques was waiting.

"I appreciate your hospitality. I promise not to cause any more trouble," Jacques said and stepped forward.

Albrecht's lips quirked up into a half smile. "You can rest in Wendell's room; I shall lay out some blankets."

Jacques nodded, grin fading as he hiked up his backpack onto his shoulder. They walked down the hall and Jacques felt eyes on him as he passed by a half-opened room. Glancing inside, he saw a man and woman glaring at him. He hurried after the kinder old man.

Albrecht pushed open the door to his grandson's room. "It's not much, but it's better than a barn or the woods."

Jacques hummed as he glanced around. "It feels warmer and looks far more comfortable." He hesitated before taking off his dirt-covered boots and placing them in a corner near the door. Albrecht brought blankets to spread out on the floor and Jacques sat with his arms around his long, lanky legs. Wendell lowered a pillow to him, averting his gaze.

"Good night," Albrecht said as he began to close the door.

"Good night, Grandfather," Wendell replied.

Jacques opened his mouth to respond, but Albrecht was already gone. He cleared his throat.

Wendell leaned over the bed, reaching for the candle set on a small table beside him.

Jacques took a quick breath. "If I may."

Wendell paused, still not facing him.

Jacques' mouth went dry, and he swallowed. "This village seems .

. . different than the others I've visited in my travels."

Wendell simply tilted his head to the side, frowning.

"Ah, my apologies, I do not mean to imply anything by it." Jacques' hands were clenched around his legs.

Wendell hummed in response. "It has been a long day. Shall we rest?"

"Yes," Jacques said, untucking himself and laying out on the thick knit blanket. He used another to cover himself.

Wendell extinguished the flame, and darkness surrounded them.

# 3

# The Bloody War

## NEW MOON

**Jacques woke up well-rested** on a pile of warm blankets. It took him a moment to remember where he was. Glancing around the room, he caught sight of blond hair poking out beneath the blankets of a heather bed. Light from the window spilled in, letting Jacques see the contents of the room clearer. There was very little furniture or personal items. Behind him was a series of drawings of the moon. The shapes went from slivers to full round circles, some filled in, some left blank. There were markings next to the drawings, but he could not ascertain their significance.

He thought of the encounter last night with Wendell, of the empty village with wary inhabitants. He wanted to ask about the legends surrounding the totems but was unsure how.

Wendell stirred on the bed, the sheets moving to show his face.

"Morning," Jacques greeted him, smiling.

When Wendell opened his eyes, Jacques squinted at what he saw.

The irises were larger and darker than they should have been, shaped differently than any he had ever seen.

"Your eyes . . ." he breathed, staring into them. Wendell sat up, leaning back against the wall, and hid his face. Jacques stumbled over his words. "Sorry, I do not mean to be rude."

Wendell was still, peering at him from beneath his bangs. "I know they are ugly; I apologize you had to see them in the light." He brushed some hair behind his ear.

Jacques shook his head. "No, they are rather unique. I've yet to see anyone with eyes like yours."

Wendell frowned. "You're not frightened of me?"

Jacques tilted his head. "Why would I be?"

Wendell scrunched up his face in confusion for a moment, then began to smile. His cheeks took on a soft rosy color. *Probably from the cold,* Jacques mused.

"Breakfast is ready!" Albrecht called from down the hall. Jacques' stomach rumbled as the fragrant cooking from the kitchen wafted in the air.

"Mmm, smells good!" he said and got up. Shivering, he grabbed his tunic from off the floor and put it on. As he grabbed for his pants, he saw bare skin and the outline of Wendell's shoulder blades as he lifted his own tunic over his head. Wrenching his head aside to give the other some privacy, he finished tying off his pants and left the bedroom.

"Good morning, Jacques. Did you sleep well?" Albrecht asked him as he entered the dining area.

"Yes, thank you again for allowing me to stay," Jacques said.

The old man gestured toward two others sitting at the table, the man and woman from last night, who gave him the same blank stares as the other villagers did. "These are Wendell's parents, Marla—my daughter—and Hansel."

Jacques bowed his head to them in deference. "I am grateful for the accommodations. My name is Jacques."

Hansel nodded back in acknowledgment, but Marla stared at him harshly. Both remained silent.

Jacques sat down where Albrecht indicated and waited. Wendell entered the room soon after. His parents did not so much as greet him. Jacques surveyed them all, curious.

"Let us pray," Albrecht said. He folded his hands in front of him, bowing his head and closing his eyes. The others did the same. "Thank you for providing sustenance for our bodies. We ask that you continue to watch over us and grant us your mercy. Amen."

"Amen," the family murmured. Jacques mouthed the words. They began eating quietly, only the clinking of silverware on plates making a sound.

"I hear a detachment of the Empire's forces was seen traveling close by," Hansel finally spoke, glancing up from his meal.

Jacques stiffened in his seat, staring at his plate intently.

"Did you see them on your way here, Jacques?" Albrecht asked curiously.

"No, sir," Jacques muttered. He stuffed a bite into his mouth to avoid speaking any further.

"Say, you look old enough to be a soldier. Have you signed up to fight?" Hansel was staring at him now. Jacques felt his face tighten and his stomach clench.

"Bah, he's far too young," Albrecht waved off the suggestion before Jacques could answer. "Although the war is not likely to end any time soon." He shook his head.

"How old are you, Jacques?" Hansel questioned him. It seemed innocent enough, but it may as well have been a death sentence by the way everyone turned to him.

Jacques cleared his throat before answering. "Twenty-three, sir."

"There is still time to enlist, then. Better to die out on the battlefield than here." Marla finally spoke. She was staring down at her plate, having touched little of it.

Jacques paused mid-bite at her words.

"Marla," Albrecht whispered furiously at her. His eyes were wide, the grip on his fork tight.

She glanced from Jacques to back down at her meal. Wendell stopped eating, his hands clenching his utensil tightly. Jacques watched him for a moment, his eyebrows knitted together. Hansel laid a hand on his wife's arm, searching her face. Eventually, she started to eat again.

"This meal is delicious," Jacques spoke up after the tension in the air became unbearable.

Albrecht smiled at him and nodded. "Thank you. We are having a good harvest so far."

"Yes, thank God for that," Hansel said. "The Lord has surely blessed us with good crops this season." He turned to Jacques with a smile. "Are you religious, Jacques?"

Jacques hesitated. With uncertainty, he swallowed and said, "I do not put much faith in a God I cannot see; besides, He hasn't helped me so far in my life, despite prayers." Disdain seeped into his voice.

The rest of the family stopped eating, staring at him with a mix of displeasure and shock. He realized he had given the wrong answer and quickly tried to rectify the situation. "Although, my family has largely been Catholic . . ."

He watched Marla and Hansel glance at each other, and his throat closed as the tension in the room rose again. As he tried to finish his meal his stomach tied itself in knots. Giving up after a few more bites, he rose slowly and gave a small bow. "Thank you for providing lodging and food to a weary traveler," he stated.

"Here, let me take your plate," Albrecht said, heaving himself up out of his chair. He jerked his head at Jacques, who followed nervously into the kitchen area.

As they cleaned the dishes next to each other, Jacques feared a rebuke or more dreaded silence. Instead, the old man talked to him in a hushed tone.

"I apologize for the conversation. The war has been on our minds recently." He paused as Jacques acknowledged the statement. "I feel it is best that you leave immediately to continue your travels. This place is not safe for you."

Jacques nodded his understanding. Everyone had said that to him so far, and he was beginning to understand why. A nonbeliever in a village full of devout Catholics was bound for peril. "Thank you for being so kind to me."

Albrecht turned to him, stopping in his motions of drying his plate. "I was once a weary traveler like yourself. I know how powerful a small act of kindness can be to ones such as us."

Jacques bowed his head to the old man. He walked back to Wendell's room without peering into the dining area. Gathering his rucksack, he made to leave without causing any more commotion.

Wendell was sitting on his bed, head dipped low. "I'm sorry about my parents," he said softly. "They've had a hard life, and may come off as unfriendly, but they're decent people deep down."

"Family can be . . . difficult, sometimes," Jacques replied. "Thank you for sharing your room with me. I won't forget the kindness you and your grandfather have shown me."

Wendell smiled at him, a bright, warm thing that softened part of Jacques' stiff limbs. "I won't forget you, either. Stay safe in your travels."

Jacques responded with a smile of his own and hesitated before adding, "Perhaps I'll see you again." Wendell ducked his head, tucking some hair behind his ear. His cheeks were pink. Jacques paused. He repositioned the pack on his shoulder. "Well, I'll be off then." They gestured a sign of farewell to each other as he left the home. Jacques glanced back as he took a few steps down the stairs. The bitter cold hit him a moment later, and he started on the dirt path out of the village as the first snow of winter came down.

"How could you say such a thing, Marla? And in front of a traveler!" Wendell's grandfather snapped as soon as Jacques was a distance off.

Wendell could hear them arguing from his room, ears sensitive to the angry tones and harsh language coming from his family's mouths. This was not the first argument he had overheard; usually, they quarreled about him. The weight of their words piled onto Wendell's shoulders, joining with the guilt and shame he felt at being such a burden. He tiptoed silently down the hall to where they were talking, glancing around the corner to watch.

His mother was glaring at his grandfather with defiant eyes. "We all know it to be true, Father," she said.

"Wendell is your son, for God's sake! Have you no compassion for him after all these years?"

His mother crossed her arms tightly over her chest, not meeting his grandfather's stern gaze. "I wanted to. I wanted to love him so badly." Wendell could see that her eyes were bright with tears. "But every month, Father. Every month we hide in our homes as that *thing*—" she choked, putting a hand to her mouth as she sobbed.

His grandfather pulled his mother into a hug. Wendell listened as she wept, wetting his grandfather's shirt with her tears and snot. His grandfather closed his eyes for a moment. He opened them and met Wendell's gaze. A silent conversation transpired between them, one of reassurance and shared sorrow. Wendell turned to walk slowly back to his room.

Wendell heard footsteps coming down the hall toward his room. The door opened with a slight creak. "Your hair is getting longer," his grandfather remarked, standing at the door. "Shall we cut it, or let it grow?"

Touching his hair, Wendell felt the lanky strands almost hanging over his eyes. "Just this part," he said. The rest had grown near to his chin, and he liked the feel of the breeze through it.

The old man nodded, taking out a pair of scissors and a comb. Wendell sat up straight as his grandfather combed his bangs forward before taking them between his fingers and snipping across to sit above his eyebrows. He went in to snip a few pieces and brushed out the excess hairs with his fingers, letting them fall to the floor.

"There." His grandfather smiled.

Wendell smiled back. "Thank you."

"I'm starting a new clock today; would you like to help?" Albrecht asked. Wendell bobbed his head up and down. They walked down the hallway, passing his parents' room. Through the half-open door, he saw his father and mother whispering to each other, hands clutching. Their gaze darted to the door as Wendell and his grandfather passed by. His father got up and closed the door as their eyes met.

Wendell lowered his head as he continued following his grandfather.

"Do not worry about them, Wendell," the old man said. "It's always rough around this time."

"Because of me?" Wendell asked with wide eyes.

His grandfather paused, sighing. He placed a hand over Wendell's head. "It is not your fault," he whispered. Wendell glanced behind them to his parents' closed door. "Come," his grandfather said. He started walking again and Wendell followed.

Albrecht's room had a table where all his clock-making tools were laid out, with thin scraps of wood from his last carving gathered in a cluster. In the corner was a walking staff with dirt still caked onto the bottom. A worn map hung on the wall, the edges curling. Stains and tears attested to its use before being pinned in place.

"You start with this part," the old man explained as he sat down, taking a small piece between his thick fingers. Wendell pulled up a chair, the feet scraping against the wood of the floor, and sat down next to him. Albrecht pointed out each piece in the process, explaining his tools and when to use them, demonstrating techniques. They worked on the clock until nightfall.

"Supper should be ready," his grandfather said, stretching. His bones cracked and popped. As he rose slowly from the chair, he exhaled loudly.

Wendell stood quickly, reaching out to help his grandfather, but pulled his hand back before the old man noticed. He took a few steps toward the door and glanced back at his grandfather.

"Go on ahead, I'll catch up," he said, his hand gripping the top of the chair tightly as he rose to his full height. "My legs are not as strong as they used to be." Albrecht chuckled and gave Wendell a reassuring smile.

The meal was silent, like most nights. A few candles lit the room as they ate, the sounds of chewing loud in Wendell's ears. No chatter about the war or bloodshed tonight.

Wendell noticed his parents glancing at each other as if making silent communication through their eyes alone. His grandfather's utensil shook slightly as it went from the plate to his mouth. Some juice from the meat dripped onto his beard, tinted red. Wendell averted his gaze. After washing the plates and utensils, he returned to his room.

The setting of the sun outside signaled it was time to leave. With a sigh, he glanced at the lunar calendar on his bedroom wall. There was a new moon out, where the normally bright sphere in the sky would be covered in darkness. He got out of his bed on quiet feet and tiptoed down the hall.

As he neared the living room, he heard the voices of his father and grandfather.

"She does love him, in her own way," his father said.

"And I love her," his grandfather replied. "She's my daughter and you are my son, there is nothing I wouldn't do for my family. But I cannot ignore the way you both speak of my grandson."

"It's difficult, this…curse." Hansel's voice was tight.

There was pain in Albrecht's voice as he replied, "Is it so difficult to love your own flesh and blood?"

Hansel gave him a solemn stare. "Yes, Albrecht. It is difficult to love a creature such as him."

Wendell flinched at his father's words, feeling as though a stake had run through his heart. Fighting back tears, he fled the house. As he made his way through the snow-covered path to the woods, windows were being latched shut tightly and candles extinguished, leaving an aching darkness in his wake. Tremors filled the air as the villagers huddled together behind locked doors. He was the only one out tonight, the crunching of snow beneath his bare feet mingling with the sounds of sharp inhalations and breathy shudders from inside the homes he passed.

# 4

# The Village Sacrifice

**Jacques shivered as he wandered** down the narrow path through the woods. Wooden bowls bumped against each other in his pack. The smell of fresh bread he'd swiped from the baker's basket only increased his hunger as he trudged onward.

A bird landed on a nearby branch, which made a dusting of snow plop onto his hair. He brushed it off, adjusting the strap of his rucksack. He thought about the strange village he was leaving behind, especially the soft blankets, warm meal, and Wendell's odd eyes.

Shaking his head, Jacques continued. The sun hung high in the sky, sweat freezing on his skin as low branches scratched his arms and tugged at his clothes. His eyes moistened as the snow thickened, bright white against the otherwise dark forest. He tripped over roots hidden beneath the white clumps on the ground, scraping his palm against tree bark. The snow was coming down in sheets, and the wind strengthened, making it difficult to move forward. Blinking rapidly and unable to keep his eyes open long enough to follow the narrow path, he soon found himself lost.

Jacques' fingers were frozen stiff, hardly able to unfurl the old, dirty parchment he had been following thus far. With no markings of the village within the forest, he had no way of knowing which direction he was headed, or whether he was simply wandering in circles. A large mound blocked his way, dark and ominous against the white snow. The skin at the back of his neck prickled, though not from the cold. His body stilled, aching to turn away, to run. It was the same feeling he had upon entering the village.

"Is there no way out of this accursed forest?" he huffed, throwing an arm across his face. His tunic was too thin to protect him from the cold and the blanket wrapped around him barely stopped the ice from seeping into his bones. His ears ached from the shrill wind and his chapped lips started to bleed. Jacques tried to retrace his steps, but his footprints were covered by falling snow. The sky darkened and he feared he would be forced to camp outside.

Jacques stumbled around for hours in circles as the falling snow continuously covered his bumbling footsteps. He leaned against a tree to catch his breath, the ragged sound abnormally loud, as the sun dipped below the forest. His ears were ringing loudly, though silence surrounded him. Even the wind had died down, with no other sounds piercing through the wilderness. He examined the area for the cause, but it was too dark. Jacques' heartbeat pounded as he took a few hesitant steps forward.

His feet hit something beneath the snow, and he fell forward. Crawling away, he brushed the white covering aside to reveal a fawn lying curled up on the ground. He wondered if it had simply frozen to death until he saw splatters of dark red amidst the white of the snow.

He inspected his surroundings and tensed. A scream crawled up his throat, but he choked it down. In front of him, a large beast was devouring the remains of an animal. Tufts of dark matted fur and the prominent outline of rib bones stood out starkly against the snow-covered bush. The sickly-sweet cloying smell of death clawed at his nose, and the low rumble of the creature's breathing made his skin tingle. He could not tell what the creature was, other than it had the shape of either a bear or a large wolf. Suddenly the odd markings on the maps in the village made sense to him; they must have been warnings about dangerous wildlife in the area.

Rising slowly, with as little sound as possible, Jacques backed away, not taking his eyes off the scene. His feet crunched atop the snow and the feasting animal lifted its head, turning toward him. Jacques stopped, not daring to breathe. The creature snorted, licking sinewy flesh and blood from its snout. Then the beast angled large, blood-stained antlers at him and charged. Jacques yelped, jumped out of the way, and scrambled through the snow. The monstrous buck struck a tree and bounced off, veering to follow him. Jacques sprinted through the woods, bumping into tree branches that tore at his tunic and stumbling over roots hidden amongst the brush. He turned back to the creature right behind him, antlers held low. His back hit something hard and he screamed as the points impaled him in the arm, lifting him up. Warm liquid trickled down his chest and he coughed, spitting up blood.

Jacques was pinned high to a tree by the points of the buck's antlers. He held onto a groove of the tines with his other hand to keep himself from being ripped open. The creature bit at his stomach and he kicked at its face. The holes in his arm stretched at the movement and he slipped further down, bark raking his back through the worn fabric of his tunic. He let out another desperate yell, pushing against the monster to free himself.

"Wendell!" a familiar voice yelled. "Let him go!"

The creature stopped ripping into Jacques' stomach. Jacques turned his head to see Albrecht gazing up at him, mouth open as he gasped. The old man took a step toward the beast and coughed, covering his mouth and backing away.

"Run..." Jacques wheezed out. He was suddenly thrown to the

ground. Blood soaked into the snow beneath his stomach. Groaning, he turned his head to watch the monster stalk toward Wendell's grandfather. Despite the pain lancing throughout his body, he was trying to protect the one person who had been so kind to him in the village. If Wendell's grandfather died out here trying to save him, he would never forgive himself or face Wendell again. His vision blurred with every breath, and his hand shook as it stretched out.

"I know you're in there, Wendell. You must stop this," Jacques heard Albrecht say breathlessly. "You do not want to wake up in the morning to the realization that you killed and ate a person you had befriended. *Please*." He saw the creature stare at Albrecht, ears swiveling in his direction as if it understood the words. "Let this traveler be," Albrecht begged. "You're better than this, Wendell, I know you are."

As he struggled to stay awake, Jacques couldn't understand why Albrecht was talking to this creature, let alone calling it by his grandson's name. "Why are you calling it … Wendell?" he gasped out.

The bizarre buck moved forward. The snow melted with a hiss beneath its hooves, turning the grass brittle and brown.

"I implore you, Nightmare. Do not do this to my grandson. He doesn't need any more reason to hate himself." Albrecht wheezed, continuing to back away at the creature's approach.

Jacques watched helplessly as Albrecht stumbled, going into a coughing fit as the beast moved closer. As it passed by him, the stench of rot wafting off the monster made Jacques' nostrils flare and his eyes sting. He saw Albrecht groan, panting for fresh air and clutching his throat.

Albrecht was speaking again, but Jacques could no longer understand what he was saying. His ears felt like they were stuffed with cotton, only rumblings coming through. His vision began to fade, and he felt himself go numb.

The cursed creature regarded the old man who dared to stand before him. Most men would run away or turn aggressive. This one did not smell of the same fear as others; instead, the spiced scent of anger filtered in through its nostrils.

"He should be dead," Wendell's grandfather whispered as he regarded Jacques. His eyes widened slightly as he gasped. "He may be the only chance we have to undo this curse!" the old man shouted before erupting into another coughing fit.

Observing the wounded man who had succumbed to unconsciousness, the creature turned away with finality. With a huff, it began stalking closer to its new prey with its head down, antlers angled for a piercing blow.

Wendell's grandfather shook his head and asked, "Will you doom us all to never-ending suffering?" There was solemnity and a grim acceptance of his fate in those words. Nothing could forestall death; neither love nor time could pause the ticking clock on each person's life.

Nightmare heard the old man's teeth grind together and saw the clenching of his jaw and fisting of his hands. "You have no regard for the people whose lives you destroy with your very presence," Wendell's grandsire seethed. The mangled buck paused to consider the words. While it could not respond in this form, it understood what Albrecht was saying. There was no need to respond, even if it could. The old man was wrong, but could never comprehend why. "You are a *monster!*" the old man yelled, then brought a hand to his mouth. Tears welled up in his eyes and shame permeated the air.

Ears flicking in anger, Nightmare turned back toward the wounded man to finish what was started. No more would this human dare to be defiant in the face of certain death.

"No, there will be no sacrifice tonight!" the elder yelled, rushing to the speared traveler who was lying still in the red-stained snow to shield him from its wrath. Tears slid down his cheeks, red streaks that contrasted against his pale skin.

But there was always a sacrifice, one way or another. Nightmare walked out of the clearing into the dense forest. The petulant fool would need to be taught a lesson: saving one person did not save them all. There would still be death this night, permanent and everlasting.

## WAXING CRESCENT

The sky was beginning to lighten with the rise of the sun. Wendell awoke. His body wracked with pain and face tight with dried tears. He saw his grandfather sitting in a chair near his bed, his head bent forward over blood-stained hands.

"Grandfather?" Wendell asked in a weary voice.

The old man lifted his head. Tears filled his eyes. "Wendell . . . oh, Wendell."

Wendell rose slowly. Dirt was smudged all over him and the blankets of his heather bed. His hair was damp, and a few small twigs were tangled in the blond tresses. Blood was caked around his mouth and encrusted beneath his fingertips. He watched his grandfather sob quietly, and then asked, "What have I done?"

The old man took a deep breath and wiped his eyes, mouth curling into a smile. "He's alive," he said with a shaky breath.

Wendell frowned. "Who is alive?"

"Jacques, the traveler who stayed the night with us. He survived the curse. It's a miracle from God!" Grandfather exclaimed, lifting his arms with eyes wide. Wendell stared at him with his eyebrows pulled together, not understanding what he was saying. His grandfather licked his lips, taking an unsteady breath. "I could tell something was wrong earlier. There were screams coming from the woods, and your father and I wondered who it could be." He inhaled sharply, hands shaking. "It was Jacques. It had to be him."

Wendell surveyed himself, lifting his hands to wipe at his face. He studied his fingers and palms, growing pale. "He was able to escape?" he asked in a hopeful tone, lifting his gaze.

Smile faltering, the elder took a moment to form the words he needed to say. "Well, not exactly. He nearly died, but I found him in time and took him to Doctor Obstein, where he'll be staying until he heals."

Wendell's face fell. He closed his eyes, clenching his hands into the sheets. His grandfather let him cry in silence.

"Would you like to go with me to check on him later?" his grandfather asked after a while.

Wendell opened his mouth, taking a breath, but stopped before any words could come out. "Should I be allowed?" he asked.

"This was not your doing," his grandfather told him sternly. "But I would not blame you for preferring not to go."

"No," Wendell said, wiping away salty tears. "I need to see what happened."

His grandfather nodded. "Get yourself cleaned up, then."

"Yes, Grandfather." Wendell rushed to the wash basin, splashing the cold water on himself to remove the dried blood and dirt clinging to his skin. He lathered and scrubbed with soap until his flesh was raw. A few stains still lingered. Wendell dipped his head in the muddied water, weaving his fingers through his hair to get the crusted dirt and grime out.

The two walked solemnly together to the apothecary. Wendell stood in front of the table where Jacques was laid, eyes bright with moisture, while his grandfather stood behind him with a comforting hand on his shoulder. Doctor Obstein was on the other side of the table, hands clasped in front of him.

"I'm a monster, just like mother says." Wendell's voice broke and he covered his mouth.

"No," his grandfather said sternly. "You were born with a curse."

Wendell sucked in a breath. "What about the sacrifice?" he asked, eyes scanning the two of them. The doctor averted his gaze. His grandfather shook his head. "If there is none, the village will suffer," Wendell stated. He examined the wounds littering Jacques' body. "And it will be my fault."

"God will forgive us," his grandfather told him. "This war has given Him plenty of sacrifices."

"I have tended to many wounded soldiers who have come through here after a battle," the apothecary added. "They have seen their own nightmares."

Wendell knew some of those soldiers had died on the village's behalf. He shook his head, his breath quickening and becoming shallow. "No, there will be consequences and it will be all because of me!" he shouted. His face went tight and red.

Doctor Obstein stepped forward, placing his hands on Wendell's shoulders. "Look at me," he ordered softly. Wendell complied, gasping for air. "Take a deep breath."

"I . . . I can't!" Wendell dry heaved, shaking. His grandfather held him tightly as Obstein took out a syringe and carefully stuck it into Wendell's arm.

Wendell woke up. His grandfather was calling out the names of his parents. With a groan, he hauled himself out of bed and out into the hall. The house was dark, the windows having never been un-shuttered from the night before. Wendell frowned, catching up with his grandfather.

The old man's feet were heavy on the old wood as he walked down the hallway and approached his parents' bedroom door. "Are you in there?" Silence greeted them. Frowning, he glanced down at Wendell before gripping the doorknob and turning.

Wendell caught sight of bare, dirty feet hovering in the air, far higher than they should be and twitching. His mouth turned down in confusion and he stepped forward.

The door was slammed shut before Wendell could peer inside. "Go back to your room, Wendell," his grandfather said shakily.

"Grandfather?" Wendell inhaled sharply, eyes dilating. "It smells like . . ." His eyes widened with desperation, then he lurched into the room. It smelled like death, that old familiar scent of dust and rot.

He was grabbed from behind and held tightly. "You shouldn't see this." The words choked out of his grandfather's mouth as he pressed his head to Wendell's back.

"No!" Wendell slipped out of the grip and went around him, stopping abruptly. The full sight of bodies hanging from the rafters hit him. "No," he whispered in a weak, high voice. In the dim light from the windows, his face scrunched up and his knees hit the floor as he keened, reaching out. His hand trembled, stopping short of his mother's frame swaying in front of him. Her eyes were half-lidded, holding neither warmth nor coldness in them. Even in death, he could not reach her.

Wendell heard the wood shift as his grandfather took a few steps forward into the room, legs wobbling a bit. With a gasp, the old man rushed toward his mother, fingers fumbling with the thick rope around her neck as he stretched up onto his toes. He took her full weight as she fell into his arms and slumped onto the floor.

"Marla . . . Marla please," his grandfather wailed, holding her close. After laying her down, he then hastily went to undo the noose around Wendell's father. The rope refused to unwind, so he searched roughly through their drawers for a knife to cut it with. Dazedly, Wendell helped by grabbing onto his father's limp legs while his grandfather stood on the stool they had used, sawing at the rope. After they brought Wendell's father down slowly next to his mother, they sobbed until Wendell's throat was sore, his cheeks tight and aching.

Their faces were discolored by the rough cords squeezed around their necks, which left angry marks against their skin. A headache began pounding against his skull.

# 5

# The Somber Ritual

**A**s the townspeople learned about the deaths of Wendell's parents, they gathered outside of their home. Wendell hid inside, sitting against the far wall of his room rocking back and forth. The chanting grew louder. He slapped shaking hands over his ears and squeezed his eyes shut. Despite that, he could still hear them shouting from outside.

"We need to rid ourselves of this wretched curse!" Bäcker hollered.

"Hand him over to die as punishment!" Fleischer demanded.

Wendell flinched at the words, his breath rushing in and out of him like a fearsome gale. They wanted to drag him from his home and hang him in the square, or stone him to death and let the wolves devour his remains. Their ire, hot and livid, filled the air. They kept their distance until now, and he wanted to flee. Constantly worrying the day would come that he was offered as the sacrifice built up a sense of dread and unease that he could never quite shake—especially in moments like these. To be hated by his own neighbors made him flinch at every glare they gave him, forcing him to be a recluse so as not to incite their hatred any further at his mere existence.

"Have you forgotten all the newborns we slaughtered before we realized it was no use? Killing Wendell will not end the curse. The next child born under a black moon will be afflicted just the same," another voice shouted over the din.

"Some of them were able to control it. Wendell is just weak!" someone else shouted. Several others from the crowd agreed, their voices rising over those who would defend him. Wendell felt sick to his stomach at their growing hostility. He wanted to run away into the woods and never come back. It was a recurring thought that he always pushed away due to the village laws and his own fearfulness of being completely alone. Now, however, it was getting harder to ignore the trembling in his legs, itching to get out of there quickly, to escape his situation once and for all.

"You would blame my grandson for this?" He heard his grandfather's voice boom above the roaring mob. Wendell crawled over to the window to see the older man's fists clenched at his sides. "If not my daughter and her husband, who would the sacrifice have been? You, Bäcker? Or you, Fleischer?" He pointed them out in the mob.

"No, the traveler!" Stuber yelled back.

"A wandering soul used as a scapegoat for our crimes?" his grandfather said, voice fierce and tinged with affront. "How many innocents must die before you atone for your own sins?"

"It's how we've survived thus far," Bäcker confessed. "We've already lost a generation from the plague. How many more must we lose?"

"If you care more for wayfarers, then leave this village and take the curse with you!" Fleischer hissed.

"You know the law passed down from our lord," Wendell's grandfather said, shaking his head. "No one can leave once they've set roots down. We cannot risk the curse spreading."

The crowd began shouting, encroaching further upon the

home with fists and household tools raised in anger. Tensing for flight, Wendell hesitated as he thought of what would happen to his grandfather should he run off. Perhaps it would be for the best— the villagers would stop harassing the older man if his nuisance kin disappeared, right?

Or they would lay even more blame on him and place *his* head on the chopping block. Wendell squeezed his eyes shut, throat closing around a sob. He had no idea what to do, and it made him ache.

"Peace, my people," a voice rang out from the group. Opening his eyes quickly, Wendell saw a clergyman appear from amongst the crowd, walking to the front. "Abraham did not hesitate to sacrifice his son Isaac when God asked him. So, too, must we commit sacrifices to appease God and lift this curse."

"How many more must be made, Father Heinrich? How much longer will this curse be held over us?" Bäcker asked.

Wendell watched the clergyman walk up the porch steps and turn to face the crowd. "That is up to Him to decide. For now, we must continue to repent of our sins and abstain from further behavior." The villagers murmured to each other, their anger finally subsiding in the face of their religion. "Now go and tend to your loved ones, for we do not know how long we will have them," Father Heinrich told them. They began to disperse. Wendell breathed a sigh of relief, his arms and legs falling limply to the side as they relaxed from their tense positions.

The door opened and Wendell's grandfather beckoned the clergyman inside. Upon seeing Wendell huddled by the window, he made the sign of the cross over himself. "I have come to perform their funeral rites," he said to the older man.

"Thank you, Father," Albrecht said in a deep, rumbling voice. The three walked down the hall in silence. The ceremony was performed in his parents' room, with them lying in bed. Wendell and his grandfather stood on one side of it while the priest recited passages from the Holy Book and blessed their corpses.

That night, Wendell and his grandfather stood on the porch together. His grandfather's face was stiff, and salt lined the crevices of his old age. The cloak he wore was thick, and the mask held in his hand would soon hide the anguish in his eyes. The villagers before them all wore the same kind of hoods and masks: the face of a stag with antlers branching upwards. The worn leather filled Wendell's nostrils. He had never thought his own family would be leading the Death March.

"Peace be among us, as the time of sacrifice has passed," Father Heinrich stated. He stood in front of them, next to the bodies of Wendell's parents lying covered on two litters made from wood and their bedding. "Today we honor the lives of Hansel and Marla Bauer, who took on the weight of our sins so that we may prostrate ourselves before the Lord. Though their deaths fill our hearts with sorrow, we can rejoice in the Lord's mercy."

"Amen," the villagers replied. Several of them came forward then, lifting each litter and lining up in rows of two on the path. Wendell's grandfather and the priest took the lead, beginning their slow walk into the forest. Wendell was left behind, as he was never allowed to participate in the burial ritual. Once they were far enough away, he snuck through the trees to watch what had always been forbidden to him.

The sky above was gray, with clouds hiding the brilliance of the stars. Snow still covered the ground, but the villagers had a steady walk. They took the bodies to a clearing untouched by nature's seasons. No grass nor snow hid the hundreds of mounds and markers. Their makeshift beds were placed down as the villagers took shovels in hand and stabbed them into the dirt. It steadily gave way until a large hole had been dug. Wendell watched as his grandfather lifted his mother's limp, heavy form off the litter and gently placed her into the ground. Beside her, they placed his father.

"The grave shall be left open for those to mourn," Father Heinrich stated. He turned to Wendell's grandfather, speaking softly so the villagers could not hear—but Wendell still could. "You shall be the one to cover them when your vigil is over."

The old man nodded. "Wendell should be allowed to be here. They were his parents."

The priest shook his head, hands folded in his sleeves. "You know he is not allowed to, for the sake of those who have died. It would be a sin for his feet to touch this sacred ground."

"They weren't the sacrifice, Father," Wendell's grandfather whispered. "I found them hanging by the neck."

"Taking one's own life is a form of sacrifice; a sin in and of itself," Father Heinrich replied. "We could not have buried them at the church with others who died of natural causes. It is against God's Will." He placed a hand on the other's shoulder. "Watch over their souls, Albrecht. I cannot say they are bound for Heaven, nor can I say they deserve to burn in the fires of Hell. May your vigil guide them to Purgatory, instead." With a squeeze, the priest walked away.

The villagers began to leave, a few at a time until the faintest sliver of the moon was high in the sky and his grandfather was left alone. Not for long, though, as Wendell stepped out from the shadows of the trees to join him. The old man and grandson stared at the bodies in silence, holding their vigil.

"I never thought it would come to this," Albrecht whispered.

"I do not understand," Wendell replied. "Why did they do it?"

"That is a question we cannot answer. The dead are silenced, unable to reveal their secrets. We can only put the blame on the curse."

Wendell was silent for a moment. His grandfather's body shook as he sobbed softly. "But the curse did not do this, Grandfather. It did not touch them."

"It touched Jacques, and yet he survived," he was told with a shaking breath. "It is because he lived that they died. You know God always takes what is due." After what felt to be an eternity of staring down into the hole where his parents now rested, never to be disturbed, his grandfather picked up a shovel and moved the upheaved dirt into the hole. Wendell took another shovel and joined him, splattering the bodies within. They were quiet as they filled the grave back up with fresh dirt. When it was done, his grandfather reached within his robe and took out a small carving in the likeness of a couple. Though simple in design, it resembled his parents enough. Initials were etched into the chests to tell them apart. He placed the marker over the dirt and stood.

After one last moment, the old man made the sign of the cross over himself and turned back. Wendell was still gazing down at the grave. His grandfather waited patiently until he finally turned to join him.

Wendell and his grandfather visited the apothecary the next day. Wendell stood at his grandfather's side as the man asked about the wounded traveler. He was staring at Jacques with guilt eating him alive from the inside out. There had to be a way for him to make up for this, to prevent his parents' death from being in vain. He had to ensure the traveler stayed alive while in the village.

"He is holding steady for now, my friend," Obstein replied.

"May we care for him at home?" Wendell suddenly asked, peering up at the physician.

Obstein studied him and gave a small smile. Tentatively, he ruffled Wendell's hair. "You wish to take care of him?" There was surprise in his voice, as well as a curious fondness that Wendell rarely heard from anyone other than his grandfather.

Wendell nodded. "It will be my penance to atone for my sins." He watched as the doctor and his grandfather exchanged glances that he could not determine the meaning of. "Please allow me to do this, sir. I need to…I need to make up for what happened to him."

His grandfather turned to him. "Are you prepared to tend to his wounds as instructed? It will not be an easy task to nurse him back to health."

"Indeed, I will need to have Katharina check on his progress," Obstein added.

Wendell nodded vigorously. "I can do it, Grandfather."

The doctor hummed in agreement. "Then I shall leave him in your care once I am sure he is recovering well. I'll send Katharina to help with his wounds. She will instruct you further."

Wendell's grandfather clasped the doctor's hand in his. "We appreciate everything you've done for us. Thank you for watching over him."

"It is a physician's duty to tend to the wounded, but I am always glad to be of help to you and your kin, Uhrmacher," Obstein replied with a warm smile. "None deserve to be cursed, but especially not your family. I am only sorry that our village has brought such ruin upon you."

Wendell wasn't completely sure what the doctor meant, but the glint in his grandfather's eyes told him how much the words meant.

"Thank you, Doctor." With a grateful nod, the old man turned to leave, gesturing for Wendell to follow.

After a few tenuous days at the apothecary, Wendell and his grandfather transported Jacques to their home, laying him down in Wendell's room on extra blankets and heather for comfort. Katharina demonstrated how to clean the wounds and replace the bandages. Wendell shuddered at the sight of Jacques' shredded skin when she removed the dark cloth wrappings. The edges around the punctures were dark and puffy, with yellow and purple bruises forming on various parts of his body. The nurse took a washcloth and dipped it into lukewarm water with drops of the tincture Doctor Obstein had made before gently cleaning each wound. She also applied a salve before wrapping the new bandages around his arm and stomach. Jacques remained unconscious throughout the process.

"Is he ever going to wake up?" Wendell asked softly, staring down at the traveler.

"His body needs rest to recover. It's a miracle from God he even survived an encounter with that monster. Give it time, Wendell," she reassured him softly. She rested a hand on his back, gently. She was the only one who had ever cared for Wendell when he was ill or wounded; he remembered her bandaging his own wounds after the older children threw rocks at him.

"Thank you, Ms. Engel," he said, daring to cover her hand with his own in thanks.

She left written instructions from the doctor and promised to return each day to monitor Jacques' healing. Wendell watched over him for a while, searching for any signs of distress; a few times Jacques' body twitched, but otherwise, he slept well. Wendell didn't sleep at all, wracked with visions of fetid leaves and the putrid stench of rot filling his nose every time he closed his eyes. His hands felt sticky with blood, and he rubbed his skin raw trying to clean them.

Supper was quiet in the evenings. Even the tinkling of silverware was muted with only two diners. Wendell glanced at the empty chairs where they usually sat. The absence of his parents hit him hard while eating. While he was not normally included in the mealtime chatter, he still enjoyed listening to the conversation. His parents' voices were usually calmer and gentler when discussing the harvest or mild town gossip. The silence was deafening now. He once wondered what it would be like with just Grandfather and him, without his parents regretting his existence. Now that it was his reality, he was disgusted at himself for ever making the wish. This was not better. This was worse. He would listen to a thousand angry rants from his mother, just to hear her voice again.

"You are not to blame for their deaths, Wendell," his grandfather said after a while of watching him push the food around on his plate. Wendell could sense the weariness and sorrow in his grandfather's tone.

"I do not feel it was a coincidence that they took their lives while Jacques lay breathing in the apothecary," Wendell replied gravely.

The air was quiet and tense. Neither of them ate, but instead clutched their utensils tightly in hand.

"You know I loved my daughter and son-in-law," Grandfather spoke through oncoming tears. "But they sacrificed more than just their lives. You must know they loved you as well, in their own way."

"They did not." Wendell kept his eyes down toward his untouched plate. "But this was the only time I ever saw them or heard their voices. Even their anger is better than this silence." He set his fork down on the wooden table, his hand shaking. "I am not hungry, Grandfather. Good night." He took his plate to the kitchen and dumped the half-eaten contents into the preserving bin. He heard his grandfather let out a shuddering breath as utensils clattered to the table.

Jacques was still unconscious when Wendell checked on him the next morning. Doctor Obstein had given him opium to help the wounded traveler sleep through the pain. The young man carefully unwrapped the bandage around Jacques' arm to reveal holes from the points of the creature's antlers. A tinge of guilt pierced him as he assessed the damage he had wrought. It was a sickening realization, seeing what his alter self could do. Wendell had seen the vicious aftermath of his monstrous curse before, but never on someone still breathing. His stomach twisted, bile rising to his throat. Clamping a hand over his mouth, he swallowed the feelings of guilt and remorse down to breathe long and slow through his nose. He had to tend to Jacques, not let himself get sick and useless. After some deep breaths, he finally settled and was able to continue cleaning the wounds.

Taking a washcloth and dipping it in lukewarm water as Katharina had done, Wendell gently wiped each section of Jacques' injured arm. After the poultice was applied, he took out new strips of cloth and slowly wrapped them around the punctures. He made them tight enough to stay in place but loose enough to allow movement and airflow, as the midwife recommended. All the while, he thought of how he could possibly make up for what he had done. The loved ones of his victims never accepted his sorrow or allowed him to express his regret. They spat at him, refusing to meet his watery eyes. Would Jacques view him with the same revulsion and hatred in his eyes as they did? The thought made him pause, swallowing down a knot in his throat. Jacques had looked at him so kindly, with no judgement or ill will, even when noticing his otherworldly eyes. To have that gaze replaced with the ones he saw every day—Wendell wasn't sure he could bear it.

Resuming his care, Wendell moved the blankets down Jacques' supine form and lifted his tunic to reveal the bandages on his stomach. Huffing, he lifted Jacques' torso, trying to be as gentle as possible. His arm trembled as it held up the other man's body while he pulled the strips of cloth free. With a grunt, he laid Jacques back down and washed the new, pale skin carefully before tying new bandages around the wound. He made sure he did everything correctly so the wounds could heal properly. Jacques had to survive this so Wendell could atone for his sins.

Jacques stirred in his sleep, his face contorting into a grimace and his limbs jerking. Sounds of pain and anguish bubbled out from him, quiet at first until they grew louder. Wendell took a step back, unsure of what to do. His heart pounded as he saw the wounded man flail in distress. Was this how he had been when he was being impaled? Crying out and thrashing around to free himself?

With a jolt, Wendell held the traveler's uninjured arm down to stop the wild movements and started cooing, "Be still, you're safe now." He moved his other hand to the dark hair, running his fingers through the short bangs until Jacques started to settle down. The skin beneath his fingertips was damp with sweat, so Wendell dipped a clean washcloth in cool water and rubbed Jacques' face and neck until his breathing evened out and he relaxed, resuming his light snoring. Wendell let out a relieved sigh and placed the washcloth by the bedside table before gathering the old, dirty bandages to discard. As he moved away from the bed, Jacques groaned in pain again.

Wendell quickly set the rags aside and returned to the bed, pulling the chair closer and sitting down to card his fingers through Jacques' hair once more. "I'll take care of you for as long as I have to," Wendell whispered to him softly. "It's the least I can do for all the pain I've caused."

# 6

# The New Family

## 1604

**R**eady to go, Elsie?" a young Albrecht asked his wife. She smiled at him, nodding. Their young daughter, Marla, was bouncing up and down, eager to go on their journey.

With only a map, some blankets, and the travel bag, the family set off from their trade city into the Schwarzwald for new adventures.

"Look at the stars, how beautiful they are out here," Albrecht said one night. They had laid their blankets out to make camp and the sky was clear.

Elsie turned to her daughter, "Do you see any shapes amongst the stars, my sweet?"

"Those ones look like a rabbit!" Marla pointed out excitedly.

"They surely do," Elsie replied, grinning from ear to ear. "I think I'll call it Marla."

The little girl giggled. She pointed at another one, "See, that one's like Daddy!"

Albrecht traced the stars she was pointing to and laughed. "Ohoho, does it now?" He scanned the night sky, humming to himself. "Well let's see, that one reminds me of a lovely young woman I grew up with."

Elsie turned her gaze to him, hiding a smile. "Oh, who would that be?"

"She's a tough one, stubborn as a mule but pretty as a mare. Might have to marry her one day."

Marla watched them, mouth in a small pout. "But Daddy, you're already married to Mommy!"

Elsie and Albrecht laughed, turning to tickle their child who cried out in glee.

"Your mother is the lovely woman I'm talking about, little one," Albrecht reassured her.

❦

# 1635

## FIRST QUARTER MOON

"Grandfather?" Wendell noticed the older man staring out of the window with a wistful expression. Curious, he approached. "What are you thinking about?" The day was beginning to wane, the sun glowing brightly against the horizon and painting the forest in gold.

With a sigh, his grandfather said, "Wendell, come take in some air with me on the porch. I have something to talk to you about." The floorboards creaked under his heavy gait. The old man eased himself down on the top step as Wendell joined him. They stared out at the village in silence. The wind was mild, with the scent of fresh bread wafting over from the baker's shop. A gust of wind ruffled Wendell's hair. It was almost to his shoulders now.

"Do you remember your grandmother?" his grandfather began in a nostalgic tone.

Wendell turned to his elder, who had a sad smile on his face that didn't meet his grandson's eyes. "I only know that she died before I was born."

"Do you know how she died?"

Wendell shook his head. He had been curious, and remembered asking as a child, but was hushed and told not to talk of such things by his mother.

"I think it's time you learned the truth." The old man gave out a long sigh and finally turned to meet his gaze. "She was killed by Loxley, the one who took on the curse before you." Wendell let out a gasp, even though he had suspected as much. Still, hearing it aloud made his throat close as bile wormed up from the pits of his stomach. Tears were forming in the old man's eyes, his mouth shaking with emotion and fists clenched on his thighs. "If I had known about the curse then, about how the villagers were trying desperately to entice travelers to stay so it would spread to others, I would have never lost her."

# 1611

After some time spent traveling, the little family stumbled upon a quaint village in the woods unlike any they had seen before.

"Welcome!" They were greeted warmly by the inhabitants. "Come stay at our inn. We have delicious food and warm beds to sleep on."

Albrecht turned to Elsie, whose face wasn't as youthful as when they first met, her hair wilder than her personality. "What do you think, my love?"

She glanced at their daughter who had grown taller and leaner throughout their travels. Marla took in the sights of the village with bright eyes. Amongst the crowd, a boy that appeared to be her age greeted them.

Elsie returned her gaze to Albrecht. "I think it's time."

They settled down in the village and Marla instantly began fawning after the farm boy she saw on that first day, Hansel. They got along like fire and wine. However, one night Marla stumbled upon some of Hansel's livestock that had been mauled to death. Her shriek alerted the two families, who came swiftly over.

"A wolf must have gotten to them!" she cried when she saw Hansel.

The boy frowned. "That was no wolf, Marla. It was the curse."

She shook her head in confusion, staring at her parents who were just as unfamiliar with the term as she was. "What are you saying?"

It was then that the new family learned about the village curse and the beast tied to the place they had come to love—and that they, too, were tied there.

"You can't leave now that you know," Hansel's father told them. "We can't have people spreading the news about a monster here. They wouldn't come to trade." He laughed it off, but the Uhrmachers were not amused. Turning to Hansel, he said, "Marry her, boy."

# 1635

Wendell ducked his head, hiding his face from his grandfather's sorrow. The thought had come to him a long time ago, but he had always hoped it wasn't true. He had wanted her death to be peaceful.

"At first, I was angry just like the other villagers. Loxley was a wolf, after all. Those vessels can be quite savage during their transformation." His grandfather's voice was low and gravelly, holding a range of emotions. "But I forgave him, eventually. He was not to blame; it was the curse, not him. I must always remember that. We all do."

"Is that why you forgive me so easily, Grandfather?"

The old man gave a slight chuckle. "You're my grandson, Wendell. I will always forgive you no matter what the beast inside you does."

"But you hate it," Wendell stated, frowning. It sometimes bothered him how his grandfather could treat him so well while also hating the curse—and by extension, part of himself.

# 1614

Albrecht paced the floor one night, wearing a trail into the old wood. Elsie had gone out during the day to fetch some supplies for the night to come, and she had yet to return.

"Where's Mother?" Marla asked, walking toward him with her arms wrapped around her. Her eyes were big, mouth pouty as if she could sense it too. It had been a few years already since they settled down. Enough to know about the curse.

"I'm going to find her," Albrecht stated, moving toward the door. Marla caught his arm. "No Father, you mustn't!"

"My Elsie is out there, and I'll be damned if—"

A wretched howl drowned out the rest of his words, the tone unsettling in its familiarity. The two grew silent and still.

"No," Marla whispered, covering her mouth. Tears were already sliding down her cheeks as Albrecht rushed forward. She let him slip through her hand.

Albrecht ran through the town past shuttered windows and tightly locked doors. Past totems of wolves and deer and horses where the curse had spawned before. They had lived in this village for years unaffected. He thought they would be lucky and escape the curse.

The sky above was black, dotted with bright stars.

Elsie's body lay down on the ground.

Hovering over her was a large beast, fur as thick as a bear's and dark as the sky above. Albrecht got closer, and it lifted its head, baring bloodied fangs and growling at him. After licking its chops, the abnormally large wolf-like creature turned away, heading back into the woods.

Albrecht dropped down on his knees, letting out a low moan.

# 1635

"I often wonder what our life could have been like had we kept going instead of settling down in this cursed place," Wendell's grandfather murmured. "I do not often regret my decisions, but I cannot stop myself from harboring hatred for the townspeople who had welcomed us in instead of warning us away. By their thinking, a new family meant new sacrifices." He looked at Wendell with warmth in his tearful eyes. "I try not to dwell on the past. Some days I wake up wishing Elsie were still in my arms." He let out a breath and smiled at Wendell. "But I have you now."

# 1617

Marla and Hansel were married in a beautiful spring ceremony. The families hoped their new life would be blessed after having been struck by the curse. New beginnings, fresh starts.

But when they learned Marla was pregnant, panic began to set in at the thought that their child could bear the curse next. Hansel paced up and down the room where Albrecht had worn a spot before, rubbing his chin. Marla sat on the couch, staring ahead with blank eyes.

"We should ask a scholar—see how close it would be," Hansel finally said.

"I'm scared," Marla whispered, her voice weak and choking around sobs. She wrapped her arms around herself as she cast tearful eyes up at him.

Hansel went to her side quickly, holding her, running his hand through her long brown hair, whispering that everything would be okay. Marla just sobbed in her husband's arms.

Albrecht frowned. "What's wrong, my child?" He came forward to sit next to his daughter, putting an arm around her.

"You know what's wrong, father. Loxley's grave was dug not long ago," Marla told him.

Albrecht's face fell as he understood—with the bearer of the curse dead, a new one was likely to be born. "I see," he said softly.

Throughout the pregnancy, Marla wrung her hands and tore at her hair. It would have been different if Loxley were still alive—if the threat of a new vessel being born was not hanging over their heads, waiting to come crashing down. They spoke with scholars who traced the cycles of the moon and the physician who monitored the child growing inside frequently.

"Even after all this time of living with it, we still cannot predict when the monster will come," Hansel said.

"The signs do not appear until the child is already born," Doctor Obstein stated. "I have examined pregnancy and birth in this village for a long time, Hansel. We simply do not have the tools and knowledge necessary to determine if your child will be cursed."

# 1635

Wendell finally understood Doctor Obstein's words to his grandfather earlier. "The villagers think our family is cursed double fold."

"The villagers are simple people," his grandfather replied without malice. "Our family is no more cursed than anyone else. It was here before I came and will remain here far after I am gone. The place itself holds the curse, I believe. But if everyone leaves, I am afraid it will wander somewhere else to inflict its chaos."

Wendell's eyebrows came together, and his lips pursed. "I thought the curse came to punish us for our sins, and that the sacrifices show repentance and faith."

Grandfather waved his hands dismissively and let out a disgruntled sound. "Truthfully, I do not believe that. God may be a cruel master, but he would not strike down a single village for such simple sins as ours. We are not Sodom and Gomorrah."

With wide eyes, Wendell asked, "Then what do you think caused it?"

His grandfather narrowed his eyes, tightening his grip on the wooden step. "That is what I wish to know, Wendell. My only thought is that it was here long before anyone else and settled here just as we have. I want to seek the answers, see if there is a cure for this madness."

"You mean leave the village?"

"Yes, but I will not leave you alone here. As much as I would like to take you with me, it is forbidden for the vessel to leave."

Wendell examined his hands. "Were you the one who suggested that law?"

His grandfather nodded. "Yes, it used to be thought that the curse was placed on the individual, so it would travel and infect other areas if those cursed were allowed to leave, so I proposed that law to our lord who sanctioned it with affirmation from the Church. Now, however," he sighed, shaking his head. "I do not know what the truth is anymore." They grew quiet, staring out into the town. "All I want is for you to be able to live a normal life, Wendell."

Wendell blinked at the old man before returning their stare to the village. He leaned slightly against his grandfather. "He was talking to me as if I were normal," he told him, still staring at the path. "Like he didn't care how odd my eyes are."

The old man's eyes crinkled up as he smiled, wrapping his arm around his grandson. "But you *are* normal, Wendell. Jacques sees it, just as I do." His grandfather held him close for a moment, filling him with a sense of calm he had desperately needed.

"I should see if he's awake," Wendell said as darkness settled around them. His grandfather nodded, and Wendell got up from the steps, smiling down at the older man before going back inside the quiet home.

# 1618

## NEW MOON

Marla screamed as pain wracked her body. Sweat covered her pale skin and her hair stuck to her face. She was sitting up, nearly hunched over. One hand clenched at the straw on the floor. Hansel clutched the other hand tightly, staring intently at her face as he watched her convulse and cry out in agony. Katharina knelt on the floor in front of Marla, using a soft voice to coax her on.

"The moon is black tonight! Is there nothing we can do to prevent this, Katharina?" Hansel asked with pleading eyes.

Marla screamed again, her voice laced with terror and knuckles white as she squeezed Hansel's hand. Squirming, her wild eyes darted around the room.

"Her labor is nearing its end, Hansel. The child comes soon," the midwife stated.

"Hold on, Marla, for just a few more hours!" Hansel told his wife, leaning closer.

She wheezed, "I-I can't!" and clamped her legs shut, knees rubbing together and feet sliding across the slick wood.

"Stop!" Katharina cried, holding her legs open.

Hansel put his other hand over his wife's. "It's not your fault," he whispered words of consolation in her ear, tears sliding down his cheeks. "We can make it through this trial, just have faith."

After a few more convulsions and horrified screams, a baby's cry filled the air.

"Ah, how wonderful, a baby boy," Albrecht cooed as he held the child in his arms, peering down at the bundle in his arms affectionately.

"What will he be called?" Katharina asked softly.

Marla was sobbing and thrashing on the floor. Hansel held her close, shaking his head.

"I think Wendell would be a good name. It's common in the family," Albrecht said, smiling at his grandson.

"That thing is *not* common!" Marla yelled.

He recoiled, eyes going wide. "How could you say such a thing about your own child?"

"That is no child of mine, it's a monster!" she wailed.

Katharina rushed to Marla's side, shushing her, and smoothed her hair back. The new mother swatted the midwife's hand away, screaming accusations of witchcraft and betrayal in her hysteria.

"Do not worry, little one," the new grandfather whispered to the baby in his arms. "I'll take care of you."

"Let me take a peek," Doctor Obstein said, holding out his arms for the babe.

Albrecht handed the child over slowly, carefully transferring the bundle from his arms to the doctor. Marla watched with a frown, face red and puffy with tears. The doctor laid the bundle on a small table, unwrapping the blanket to reveal a small baby boy.

"His face is not long like the horse, nor does he appear to have hooves," Obstein commented as he examined the baby. He lifted the child's upper lip with his finger to reveal soft, pink gums. "It is too soon for the fangs of the wolf to come in."

The baby squirmed on the table, opening its eyes to reveal an abnormally large iris of dark brown with an oval-shaped pupil. They stared back at the doctor, who leaned back.

"His eyes, doctor…" the father whispered.

"Ah, yes, the mark of the deer."

# 7

# The Perilous Fever

## WAXING GIBBOUS MOON

**The wounded traveler was perspiring** despite the chilly air, unruly bangs sticking to his slick forehead. Taking a clean wash rag, Wendell dipped it in cool water, rung it out, and applied the damp cloth to Jacques' head. The rag got warm quickly. Frowning, Wendell began to unwrap the bandages around the traveler's arm. Yellow, thick liquid came out of the punctures, while the edges were still dark and puckering. Jacques' arm was rounder than before—swollen—with the wrappings tight enough to leave marks against his skin. Wendell placed his hand on Jacques' forehead, feeling the heat radiating against his palm.

He sat up straight, searching the wounded man for more clues. Jacques' breathing was haggard, and his fingers were clammy, while his eyes moved rapidly beneath the lids.

"Grandfather!" Wendell called, panicking. He was going to lose Jacques just like he had lost his parents; the touch of death always surrounded him.

The floorboards squeaked as the elder arrived quickly, each step becoming louder until the door swung open. "What is it?"

Wendell whirled around to face him, eyes large. "Fetch Katharina, there's something wrong with Jacques," he breathed out.

Katharina came quickly, carrying her bag of instruments and remedies. Wendell and his grandfather stood back as she examined Jacques. She touched his skin and gasped, stepping back. "His body is emanating heat!" She turned to Wendell. "Did you feel this too?" Wendell nodded, wringing his hands. She made the sign of the cross over herself. "My God, Nightmare's touch has done this."

Wendell's mouth dried up and his eyes prickled with tears. Despite his best efforts and hopes, it seemed that Jacques was going to die from the curse anyway.

"Has this happened before?" he heard his grandfather say beside him. "A slow death after one has encountered the curse?" he clarified.

Katharina shook her head, staring at Jacques with wide, horrified eyes. "No, death has always been instant. Even the flora and fauna are afflicted without time to restore life. It is part of the curse."

"Is there anything we can do?" his grandfather asked solemnly.

Wendell stared at Jacques' face as the wounded traveler winced and panted. He couldn't bear to watch the traveler die and began to turn but stopped when he saw his parents' closed door. Eyes meeting Jacques', he swallowed back bile and clenched his fist.

Katharina unwrapped the bandages around Jacques' arm. "Normally he would be bled to get the toxins out, but he has already lost so much blood from the wounds, it would be dangerous to take any more," she said. Putting her fingers to the inside of his wrist, she stood there for a moment as the two watched nervously. "His heart is beating too fast; it is generating heat. We must slow it down or find another way to release the bad humors."

She unpacked her bag, taking out vials of liquids and dried herbs. "I will try to remove the cause, but it may take some time to work," she told them. "How long has he been like this?"

"When I cleaned the wounds earlier, they were swollen and discolored. He was sweating then, too. I thought maybe . . . it was part of the healing process," Wendell murmured, rubbing his arms. He hoped it wasn't too late. There were very few books about medical practice in the town hall, so his knowledge was slim. He told himself that he could not have known, as he was not a health practitioner like Obstein and Katharina, but the guilt still threatened to consume him whole.

She nodded. "It must have occurred overnight, then." Katharina ground up coriander seeds and mixed them with a clear liquid that Wendell could not identify, then coaxed Jacques' mouth open to pour the potion down his throat. "Help me turn him onto his side, else he will choke on his expulsions," she asked. Wendell rushed forward, being careful not to jostle the wounds as he worked with Katharina to move Jacques onto the side. "Albrecht, grab an empty bucket," she ordered.

Wendell heard his grandfather go down the hall and shuffled some items around before quickly coming back with a small bucket. Jacques was groaning, his skin slick with sweat and shivering as if cold. Goose pimples blotted his body while the small hairs on his arm stood up. Eventually, he began to vomit into the bucket, though it was mostly liquid. Wendell grimaced, his nostrils flaring with his sensitive smell overwhelmed by the sour stench.

When nothing more came out, they rolled Jacques onto his back and Katharina wiped his mouth with a damp cloth. She then doused a separate rag with a strongly scented yellowish liquid and used it to clear off the puss oozing from the wounds.

"What is that?" Wendell asked, scrunching up his abused nose from another onslaught of sour fragrances.

"Vinegar," she replied. "It will help kill the fever." She kept using the vinegar-soaked rag to clean the punctures and then wrapped them in new, fresh linen. Jacques gave out a few moans but remained unconscious. "He needs to be closely monitored for the rest of the day until the fever breaks. I'll leave the vinegar with you; clean and change out the bandages more often. I will be back first thing tomorrow to check on him."

"Thank you," Wendell said softly.

Katharina paused and turned to him, silent for a moment as she studied Wendell with knowing eyes. "It is quite like the cervine to care for a sick member of its group. You may be the monster's host, but you are nothing like that beast. Please remember that, Wendell."

Wendell's eyes widened and he opened his mouth to speak but did not know what to say. Gratitude overtook him. Someone else cared for him aside from his grandfather, and the compassion shown caused his eyes to water. His throat ran dry and he swallowed.

His grandfather chuckled. "How is it that you and Doctor Obstein are the only ones besides myself who care for my grandson?"

"It does not take much effort to be kind to others, Albrecht," she replied, turning back to her patient as she continued. "Your neighbors are scared and angry because the curse is still unknown to them. But to myself and the good Doctor, it is simple." She placed her vials and herbs back into her bag carefully, the sounds of clinking glass muffled from inside. "Much like I can separate the disease from an individual, I can separate the curse from the cursed. It was the same with Loxley. Despite the terrible things he had done due to the curse, I never thought of him as my enemy or someone to be hated. If anything, I pity those who are directly affected by the curse. You are the ones who suffer the most."

"It's good to hear someone speak so plainly about it. I fear the rest of the townspeople will never understand the curse," his grandfather said with a shake of his head. Wendell listened in a haze, still attempting to comprehend the emotions he was feeling. Their words were dampened as if far away, even though they were standing right next to him.

Katharina lifted her shoulders. "It is human nature to fear what one does not understand." Turning to Wendell with a bowl in hand, she asked, "Please fill this with fresh water."

Snapping out of the haze, Wendell took the bowl without a word and rushed down the hall, out of the door, and over to a spigot. As he waited impatiently for the water to fill the bowl, he sensed another presence nearby. He noticed the innkeeper staring at him with narrowed eyes.

"Mr. Stuber..." Wendell said hesitantly. The thin man did not respond, only squinted at him as the water kept pouring from the spigot. Stuber's fists were clenched at his side. Water splashed as the bowl overflowed. Wendell hastily stopped the spigot and picked up the bowl, its contents sloshing onto the ground and his feet.

"You don't belong here," Stuber growled as Wendell hurried back inside, careful not to spill more of the water. He was breathing heavily by the time he came back to the room. When Katharina took the bowl from him, his hands were shaking.

"Your face is pale, Wendell. Are you ill as well?" she asked, placing a hand on his forehead.

Wendell's skin felt cold, but he knew it was not from sickness. "No, just . . . Mr. Stuber was outside."

His grandfather frowned. "What did he say to you, my boy?"

Wendell started shaking his head, the contrast of Katharina's unusual kindness with the innkeeper's standard animosity clashing within in his mind. "He said . . . that I didn't belong."

The old man's expression darkened as he made to leave, but Katharina laid a hand on his arm. "Steady, Albrecht. More harm will come from you acting against him. Let us continue tending to Jacques." Taking a deep breath, Wendell's grandfather settled, nodding in agreement.

She placed the dirty cloths in the bowl until the water became brown. Wendell took the bowl and dumped it outside once the cloths were thoroughly rinsed, glancing around. The innkeeper was gone, but an ominous feeling still crept across Wendell's skin.

Once all of Jacques' wounds were treated, Katharina turned to them. "The fever will keep him asleep, but the rest should help speed up recovery. Try to get him to drink water as often as you can."

"What if he still doesn't heal?" Wendell asked.

"That is a mystery in itself," she replied. "I am curious about his condition as well, but the most I can do now is treat it as best as I know how." Wendell nodded slowly, wrapping his arms around himself and biting his lower lip. "If my methods do not work, we may need to call upon others who have experience in dark magic and divine miracles."

Wendell's grandfather glanced at the midwife. "You mean an Inquisitor?" he asked with wariness in his tone. Wendell's eyebrows furrowed in the center as he discerned what they were talking about. He had not heard the term 'Inquisitor' used before.

"Yes, perhaps the Church would know why this young man survived the curse," Katharina replied.

"You think him to be a witch?" Wendell's grandfather was incredulous now. Wendell was more curious about his tone than the accusation, only hearing about witches in hushed tones from other villagers.

Jacques began to stir, groaning.

"He is in pain. Wendell, please come here," Katharina gestured him over. "Take his hand and squeeze lightly."

Wendell did as he was told, keeping his eyes locked on Jacques' face. The injured man slowly relaxed and his breathing finally calmed. Wendell stayed with him, barely moving, for the rest of the day.

Sunlight filtered into the room from the small window near the bed, hitting Wendell's face and leaving his skin warm. He woke up blinking against the brightness and noticed that his fingers were wrapped around Jacques'. His cheeks warmed and he retracted his hand quickly, heart beating wildly. Jacques' breath was slightly labored, but his pallor was better than the day before. Wendell checked for signs of the fever, pursing his lips at how warm the traveler's skin remained under his touch.

He smelled pork and heard sizzling sounds coming from the kitchen. Reluctantly, he left Jacques' side and trudged into the dining room. Albrecht brought plates of bacon and eggs to the table, smiling at Wendell as he set them down.

"Did you sleep well?" his grandfather asked with a crinkle in his eyes. Wendell hummed and nodded, yawning. He dug into his food eagerly. His grandfather chuckled. "I went to fetch you for dinner, but you had fallen asleep at his side."

Wendell felt his cheeks warm and ducked his head. "I didn't want to leave him alone," he whispered.

The elder pat his shoulder. "You are doing well by him, caring for him like this. I'm proud of you, Wendell."

Wendell felt his chest swell with gratitude and smiled at his grandfather.

Katharina kept her promise, returning over the next few days to confirm that the fever was reducing. Jacques woke a few times, eyes bleary and speech jumbled. They could barely understand him as he slurred his words together.

"He is delirious. The fever is making his mind fuzzy," she explained. "But fret not, he is recovering steadily with this regimen. Just stick to it for a few more days, and he'll be on the way to full health."

"Will his wounds leave a scar?" Wendell asked tentatively. He hoped she would have a potion or curative up her sleeve to lessen the appearance of the large gashes. Every time he saw the wounds, he thought of how terrifying it must have been to receive them. It made him sick.

"As deep as they are, there will most likely be scarring after the punctures seal up." At Wendell's sorrowful expression, she added, "Do not view them as reminders of the pain you caused—but of his survival. They are marks to prove he lived through an attack from Nightmare. This is a good thing."

"Have you discovered any clues as to how he survived?" his grandfather asked.

"No, but Doctor Obstein and I have many thoughts about it." Katharina sighed. "It could be that only the village is cursed so that travelers from across the land are not affected by the normal decay that comes with its presence—but we have seen outsiders be chosen as sacrifices. Or it could be that Jacques is immune somehow." The old man's expression grew hopeful, but the medicine woman did not. "However, our examinations have not provided any signs that Jacques is different from the rest of us. We cannot know for sure, as there are too many possibilities. Perhaps when he is well again, we can assess him further to determine the exact cause."

Wendell frowned. "Would it hurt him?"

"I am unsure," Katharina replied honestly. "I simply wish to ask him questions of his origin. He may have the answers we seek."

Wendell tilted his head slightly, still staring at Jacques with a crease in his brow. What answers could this stranger hold to unlock the secrets of a generations-long curse afflicting only their tiny village?

# 8

# The Mysterious Curse

## FULL MOON

**Jacques woke suddenly, realizing he** was alive as he took in the sight of the wooden ceiling. There were soft blankets on his skin, and the smell of food lingered in the air. He tried to move, wincing in discomfort and finding his limbs stiff, so decided to stay still. The pain began to catch up to him, making him grit his teeth and squeeze his eyes shut as it washed over like a harsh breeze. When he opened them again, he saw bandages wrapped around his arm and abdomen. Soft heather was beneath him—a bed. Jacques studied the room, recognizing the lunar drawings on the wall and noticing clean bandages along with different vials lined up on the bedside table beside him.

"I am so sorry," a voice murmured beside him, making Jacques twitch in surprise, then hiss in agony at the fast movement. Wendell's grandfather was sitting in a wooden chair near the bed, elbows on his knees and head down. He sounded far older than when he was yelling at the creature in the woods.

"What are you apologizing for?" Jacques asked, struggling with the effort to speak. His throat was hoarse and his head fuzzy. Everything ached, from his legs to his arms to his stomach. Even his back was sore from the tree bark digging into his skin and the impact with the ground. "You saved me. I owe you my life." The older man stayed silent. Jacques recalled Albrecht's argument with the creature that had tried to kill him. "How did you do it?" he asked quietly, curiously.

Albrecht glanced to the doorway. Jacques' eyes followed the old man's gaze, seeing Wendell. His head was tilted down to where Jacques couldn't see his face.

"There are some things we need to tell you about this village, Jacques," Albrecht stated solemnly. "But please know that it is not Wendell's fault that you were harmed."

Lying his head back down on the downy pillow to relieve the strain on his neck, Jacques stared at the ceiling and let out a feeble sigh. "I'm not sure what happened . . . but how could it be related to Wendell?" He turned his head, waiting for an answer.

"The village is cursed," Wendell finally spoke up, eyes meeting Jacques'.

"Cursed?" Jacques blinked, lips downturned and eyebrows coming together.

"Yes," Albrecht replied. "About every generation, a child born under the new moon is forced to transform into a terrifying creature and take on the curse themselves. We call this creature Nightmare."

Jacques stared at them, not understanding a word they were saying. He did not believe in monsters and fairy tales. What attacked him in the woods—it had to have been some wolf or bear, right? Why were they making up a story about curses and nightmares? "Is this some form of jest? Are you mocking me?" Anger flared within him briefly at the thought.

Wendell and Albrecht shared a pointed look. "I assure you, what we are telling you is the truth," Albrecht said.

The old man nodded at his grandson, who took a deep breath. "When I was ten years old, I transformed for the first time. The villagers thought they could keep me locked in the cellar since I was born with the mark of the deer. They thought my cursed form would be docile enough—or that I could control it somehow." He shuddered, swallowing.

Albrecht continued for him. "But we discovered that one cannot keep death bound or waiting."

"Nightmare is what attacked you," Wendell said, his strange eyes shiny with tears. He choked on his next words. "I'm sorry. I have no control over myself in that form, I barely remember anything that I've done, I can't—"

"Woah, slow down," Jacques said as Wendell began speaking rapidly. "What do you mean?" He examined their expressions, still unable to understand the implications of their words.

"Wendell was born on such a night," Albrecht explained gently as if talking to a student. "He was burdened with a curse that demands monthly sacrifices."

Jacques stared at Wendell curiously. His brain sluggishly worked on the connection between Wendell, a stag, and the curse, but only produced a sharp pain in his head. "That makes little sense. I'm sorry, but how can that be?"

Albrecht and Wendell glanced at each other again, both frowning. Jacques couldn't read their expressions, but he knew a silent conversation was happening between the two.

"You should rest more, it's not the right time to discuss this matter, it seems," Albrecht said, standing. He beckoned Wendell to follow him out of the room, turning back to Jacques with a somber expression.

"Am I dreaming?" Jacques whispered to himself once they had gone. Even though he tried to figure out what they were saying and whether it was true, he soon drifted back to sleep.

Jacques awoke after what he assumed were a few hours of unconsciousness. Wendell sat in the rocking chair with a book on his
lap. "Wendell?"

Wendell's head lifted when Jacques called out to him. He smiled
and set the book aside. "You're awake again."

Jacques glanced down at the cloth surrounding his arm and torso to confirm his condition; still skeptical about everything that happened. His hand moved to tentatively touch the wrappings on his
stomach. "How long was I asleep?"

"Just a few hours," Wendell replied.

"And before that?" Jacques asked with strain in his voice. "How
long has it been since . . ." He gestured to his wounds.

Wendell picked up a scroll on the table with a set of tally marks.
"You've been recovering for about two weeks."

Jacques' eyebrows rose. "That long?"

"You had a fever for a few days," Wendell explained, pointing to
one set of tally marks. "Katharina has been tending to you. I should
fetch her and the doctor." He got up to leave.

"Wait," Jacques called out to him. His mind was beginning to
clear, and the ache in his limbs grew dull. But he needed to know if the
discussion he remembered having with Wendell and his grandfather
was a hallucination or not.

Wendell sat back down in the chair with an expectant expression.

Wetting his lips, Jacques asked warily, "So that creature . . . the
curse . . . it's all real?" He half expected Wendell to think he had concocted it out of some delirium, but instead the other nodded, glancing
away while biting his lip.

Jacques stared up at the ceiling, swallowing. He closed his eyes
and took a deep breath. His dreams had been haunted by the beast

in the dark woods. He had wished they were just his wild imagination from traveling. Now he was faced with reality.

"I used to hear stories of people who could turn into monsters," Jacques said after a moment of silence, face pale and eyes unfocused as he rationalized the story they had told him. "They were just legends told around campfires to scare people. In the towns I went to, bards would craft these kinds of tales for hours and accept tips in exchange to buy some bread. I never thought they were true—just made up for entertainment. The only people who believed the bards' stories were outcasts, town drunks, and strange people who practiced magic in the trees."

"They're not just stories, here," Wendell murmured.

"All right," Jacques said to himself. If this was his reality, then he would face it head-on. He met Wendell's eyes. "Tell me more."

The young man shifted, eyes darting around the room. He fiddled with the book. "What do you want to know?" he asked after a moment.

Jacques remembered the first thing he noticed when he entered the village. "The things hanging up all around the village. They've got bits and pieces on them."

Wendell tilted his head as if thinking. "Oh," he said, straightening. "Those are totems; they symbolize the curse's many forms. Some villagers think they provide protection, while others use them to mark spots where the curse has struck." Jacques listened carefully as Wendell spoke, enthralled with the explanation. His arm throbbed, reminding him of the creature's brutality, yet he couldn't find it in himself to blame the person in front of him. "From what we know, Nightmare is a being that lives on through other people. It takes on three different forms, depending on the vessel: a horse, wolf, or deer. Of the three, the wolf is usually the most dangerous. They are powerful and intelligent but tend to be more violent and extremely loyal to those who care for them. Every new moon, they become large wolves that are bigger than our cattle.

"Those born of the horse are kind and hardy yet tend to be wild and unpredictable. They turn into beasts that stand taller than our workhorses, with a deadly horn coming out of their forehead. When they leap, it's almost as if they're flying." Wendell paled. After a moment, he muttered, "The deer is generally the nicest and least threatening, while human. Although most villagers say they are the most terrifying when transformed. We have depictions of them from previous generations, and they all horrify me." He was rubbing his arm absently, glimpsing to the side of Jacques instead of directly at him.

Jacques felt a shiver go down his back as goosebumps appeared on his skin. The creature that attacked him was certainly the most frightening thing he had ever seen. "And you transform into that thing?" Wendell nodded, picking at his fingernails. Jacques was silent for a while, imagining the creatures that Wendell had just described. The young man's shy nature was certainly a stark contrast to the way that thing behaved. "How long has it been haunting the village?" Jacques asked, straining to turn more toward Wendell.

"No one really remembers when it all started," Wendell told him, shifting around in the chair until he was more settled in. "The historical scrolls we have began documenting the existence of the curse a couple of hundred years ago. But Grandfather and I think it's been here for much longer."

They were quiet for a while. Jacques moved to a more comfortable position and breathed deeply as the pain edged further into his awareness. Just as he was about to ask Wendell about medicine or the doctor, the door opened to reveal Albrecht.

"Ah, Jacques, you're back with us. Are you hungry?"

Jacques felt his stomach tighten, empty and wanting. "Yes, very much so."

Albrecht's face brightened. "Well, it's good I came to tell Wendell that lunch is ready, then. I'll bring you a plate and fetch the doctor."

"Thank you," Jacques said, meeting their eyes, "for caring for me."

Their faces clouded over. "It's the least we can do for what was done to you," Albrecht said.

Wendell fed Jacques warm oxtail soup and berries as Albrecht left to call upon the doctor. He returned with Obstein and Katharina as Jacques finished lunch.

"How are you feeling?" Doctor Obstein asked. He placed his hands on Jacques in various places near his wounds and put his ear over his chest for a moment.

Jacques grimaced, inhaling sharply. "Hurts," he exhaled. Sitting up to eat the soup made his arms achy—they started shaking halfway through the meal—and his midsection ached.

"I have a tincture for the pain. You may feel tired, but your body needs rest most of all to heal," the doctor replied and picked up a vial of dark liquid. He held it over Jacques' open mouth, letting a few drops spill out. "I need to check your wounds to ensure they are healing properly." Jacques nodded, swallowing down the tincture and willing his body to relax. The doctor unwrapped the stained cloth as he watched, and his eyes widened at the extent of the damage. "They appear to be closing nicely," Obstein said as he watched Jacques carefully.

"Yes, I've noticed a steady improvement in their appearance over the past few days," Katharina added.

The pain slowly began to ebb away as the doctor treated his arm. A cool cream was applied to the punctures; an odd sensation Jacques did not think he would ever get used to. He tried not to use or move the injured arm much, as it throbbed when he did so. His breathing was steady by the time the doctor began unwrapping his stomach bandages. Jacques had to close his eyes, swallowing a tangy remnant of soup when he saw the sinewy tissue where his skin should be.

"Relax," Katharina said softly. "You are recovering well."

Jacques forced his body to unclench from the stiff posture, exhaling loudly. His midriff was sore to the point where each breath was painful. Obstein applied the cream to the exposed sections of Jacques' abdomen from the creature's gnawing. Then Katharina wrapped new bandages around him as the doctor stepped aside, whispering to Albrecht and Wendell who had been watching from the doorway.

"You are very brave," Katharina murmured, drawing Jacques' attention.

"I'm not sure brave is the right word," Jacques said a bit breathlessly.

"Strong, then?" the midwife smiled at him. "You are the only one to have survived an attack from Nightmare."

Jacques remembered the fawn he found lying in the snow, the nauseating smell, and Albrecht coughing the night he was attacked. Death surrounded the curse; so why did he survive? "I know not why," Jacques admitted. "Or even how."

Katharina's hands were soft and gentle. "There are still many things we do not know about the curse that plagues our village. I hope we can come closer to finding the answers while you are here."

Jacques' lips quirked up into a smile at her and his gaze slid to Wendell, who was paying attention to the doctor intently, hands clasped together so hard his knuckles were pale. He saw Albrecht place a hand on Wendell's shoulder, who turned to him. His gaze caught on Jacques, though.

Jacques' eyes were heavy as they stared into Wendell's. Darkness crept around the edges of his vision until those large, dark irises were the last thing he saw before falling asleep.

## WANING GIBBOUS

As Jacques continued to recover, Wendell found himself talking to the traveler more and more.

"When I was young, I learned how to run away from the rocks other children threw at me," Wendell told Jacques after he had asked about the way the villagers acted. He had tried his best to ignore the hurtful words that came with them.

Jacques frowned at him with worry. "That must have been awful growing up with."

Wendell nodded at him, remembering how cruel the other children had been to him.

"I have been a pariah my whole life," Wendell explained. "The villagers would blame everything on me, from their crops failing to animals dying, the weather turning bad, and even the war."

Jacques remained silent; eyebrows furrowed. He swallowed, giving Wendell a sad expression. Wendell glanced away, lacing his fingers together and twisting them out of nervousness. It was strange, to tell someone from outside of the village this information. The only one who would listen to him before was his grandfather, who had witnessed these things happen. He wasn't sure how to convey the awful way the people had treated him his whole life and the confusion he felt until he was old enough to understand why. Even now, he did not begrudge the children who feared the monster within him, or the adults who turned away as he passed by them.

"I bet there are others like you out there," Jacques finally spoke.

Wendell blinked, drawn out of his thoughts. "What do you think happens to them?" His eyes fixed on the floor.

In his peripheral vision, he saw Jacques tilt his head to the side. "What do you mean?"

"Do," Wendell paused, pursing his lips. "Do people hate them? Like the townspeople here hate me?"

Jacques' expression turned grim, and his lips formed a thin line across his face. "Maybe," he said honestly. "People are afraid of what they do not know or understand. Stories of monsters killing townspeople have probably turned fear to anger in some."

Wendell thought about little Wilhelm and the way his gray-haired mother always glared at him. He curled inward, resting his chin on his knees.

Jacques leaned closer, putting more pressure on his stomach, but Wendell remained silent and distant despite their physical closeness. After a moment, the wounded man settled back against the feather pillows propped up against the wall and let out a huff of breath. "It's not . . . I don't blame you for what happened. It was ill-advised of me to go running around in the woods at night. I just . . ." His lips pursed.

Wendell watched Jacques, breath catching in the back of his throat. Jacques' mouth was slightly open. His eyes slid to Wendell's and then to the wall in front of him.

"I wanted to see you again," Jacques finally admitted. His expression was as raw as his injuries.

Wendell drew in a sharp breath, feeling his cheeks heat up and his heartbeat increase. He could not think of words to say in response for a moment. A smile wound its way across his face as he tucked a stray piece of hair behind his ears. "I wanted to see you again too," he said softly.

Jacques let out a breath as if he had been holding it in all this time and then chuckled. Wendell's smile widened.

A distinct creak of wood in the hallway drew Wendell's attention to the door. He listened to the familiar sound of his grandfather's heavy gait as it moved down the hall. The closer he got to Jacques, the farther away his grandfather seemed.

Jacques was able to join them at the table for dinner after a few more days. He was growing restless lying in Wendell's bed all day and night.

He stretched lightly before Wendell guided him down the hall as his legs adjusted to walking again. A bit wobbly, he hobbled forward slowly and used one hand against the wall to manage his weight.

There were three place settings on the table. Jacques glanced around the room. "Are your parents not joining us?" he asked. Jacques realized he had not seen Marla or Hansel during the time he was recovering. Nor had Wendell or Albrecht mentioned them.

The two grew tense, their faces shifting as they avoided his curious eyes. It was Wendell who answered him. "They're . . . gone."

Jacques blinked, jerking back. "What happened?" he asked. Where could they have gone during this time? Did they leave because of him? He remembered their shocked faces when he announced he was not religious the first time they had dined together.

Wendell opened his mouth and then shook his head, putting his face in his hands. Albrecht spoke instead. "They died the same night you were attacked."

Jacques' mouth went dry. He avoided Albrecht's stone expression to see Wendell's shoulders shaking. "I'm," his voice cracked, and he cleared his throat. "I'm so sorry."

Albrecht nodded, murmuring his gratitude at the thoughtfulness. The rest of the dinner was silent. Jacques felt like a heavy boulder was placed between his shoulder blades, teetering on the edge of his spine and neck and threatening to squash him underneath at any moment.

# 9

# The Unwanted Child

## QUARTER MOON

## 1623

**G**et away from here!" one child yelled, hurling a stone at young Wendell who had asked to play.

Wendell let out a cry and covered his head with his arms as more children arrived. They picked up large stones and threw them at him.

"We don't want to play with the village curse!"

Wendell dropped to the ground from the onslaught, crying out every time a rock hit his tiny body.

"Stop that!" A booming voice called out over the uproar. Wendell's grandfather ran forward and knelt next to his grandson as the others scattered. "You poor thing. Why didn't you call for me?"

# 1625

## WANING CRESCENT MOON

Wendell heard excited shouts and cheers from the streets as music played in the distance. The smell of sweets and fresh meats wafted through the air from the open window. "Momma, Papa, what's that?" he asked, turning to his parents.

They didn't answer him or acknowledge his question. It was his grandfather who came up to him, kneeling beside him and watching as people passed by with carts full of goods. "It's a festival. The village hosts one every year around this time."

Wendell's eyes widened, focusing on the new faces and unfamiliar items he saw them carrying. His grandfather must have noticed because he asked, "Would you like to go?"

"Absolutely not," his mother suddenly hissed. She was surveying them now with sharp eyes. "You know he is not allowed to participate."

"Nonsense, he's just a boy! Let him have fun," his grandfather replied jovially.

Wendell turned his large, irregular eyes onto his mother. "Can I please go, Momma?" he begged.

She huffed, getting up abruptly from where she sat, throwing her knitting needles on the floor, and stomping away down the hall. Wendell's father shook his head. "I would not advise such a venture, Albrecht."

"Why should he be excluded when he is still a part of this village? Wendell has done nothing wrong. I'll be there by his side."

His father sighed, rubbing his forehead. "I suppose he can go while he's still young. But if anything happens . . ." he said with a warning tone.

"I will ensure he is not harmed," Wendell's grandfather replied. His father glared at the elder. "And of course, that no one *else* is harmed."

Wendell smiled wide at his grandfather as the older man took him by the hand and led him outside. They joined the throng of newcomers down the path toward the center of town.

"It's a fine day for a celebration," Grandfather commented as they walked. While still a bit cold, the air was crisp and refreshing. The sun peaked out amongst the clouds, warm against Wendell's skin. The young boy admired all the new sights and smells with a gleeful step, grinning at everything.

As they got closer, the sounds of laughter, cheers, and stomping got louder. Wendell could smell pork roasting and the spice of cider.

"They must be dancing," his grandfather said.

"Dancing?" Wendell asked, hurrying forward to see what he meant. The old man pointed to a group of men clad in lederhosen who were slapping their thighs and knees, singing while others played instruments behind them. Wendell watched in awe as they jumped around and shouted to the tune of the music.

His grandfather watched with a warm smile, but they didn't miss the glares being sent their way. A few people took steps toward them to interfere, but the older man stood in their way, meeting the angry stares with one of his own, challenging them.

"He shouldn't be here," one of the villagers said.

Wendell's attention was pulled away from the dancers to the townspeople around him who had angry eyes.

"He has every right to enjoy the festival as you do," his grandfather replied. "Leave him be, unless you want to cause a fuss with travelers around and ruin the merriment of the day."

"Watch that he doesn't scare them all away," the villager grumbled. With that, the townspeople walked away from them, leaving a wide berth.

# 1628

## NEW MOON

The dark shape of the moon had risen high into the sky, indistinguishable from the stars. The transformation began and Wendell cried out. His head throbbed and he clutched it as two sharp points jutted through his scalp. Small, hard bumps broke through the skin, causing warm blood to drip down his face. His headache turned into a nauseating migraine.

The bones in his limbs cracked and he screamed and fell. His skin grew taut, stretching thin in places where his legs elongated, and his knees bent backward. His arms shook with the pressure, fingers popping and cracking as they turned into large hooves. Bile burned a path to his throat until he vomited onto the cold cellar floor. Sobbing, his tears mixed with the blood coming from his face. His jaw extended and gore dripped out of his mouth.

Pelt emerged over his skin, his ribs cracked as they displaced themselves, and then the sensation started to become distant. His vision blurred and senses dulled; it felt like falling asleep as he lost control of his movements. His panicked thoughts died down, replaced with a calm, instinctual urge.

Nightmare stood on four shaking hooves where Wendell had been huddled. Heat wafted from its body, with blood matted into its dark brown coat and thick red drool dripping onto the floor. The newly formed creature observed the stone walls, breathing roughly. Long ears twitched, taking in the sounds of hushed discussion just above. Its eyes drifted up to the ceiling where a conversation could be heard.

"Are you sure about this? Others have broken out before. We have no way to keep the monster in place."

"Maybe it won't be as bad as Loxley. Maybe Wendell can control it."

"Have you ever seen a buck charge?"

A hush came over the room and the air changed from mild panic to growing terror. The creature's nostrils flared as it huffed, tasting their fear on its tongue. It took a steady step forward on its hooves. The room Wendell was locked in had been lit by a few candles on the walls, which sputtered out as Nightmare stalked forward onto the staircase. The points of its antlers scraped against the ceiling and a shrill grating sound broke the silence as the structure began to crumble with age.

"Do you hear that?"

"Hear what?"

"He's stopped screaming."

"Is it over?"

The animal's antlers were too tall for the entryway, so its head bent forward. It backed up and then shoved them against the door.

The building shook, the air growing thin and dusty.

"What is that?" a villager whispered. A crack formed in the door from the impact of Nightmare's antlers. It heard the floor creak beneath footsteps that receded from the doorway.

"It's coming," another villager breathed shakily. "Grab a weapon!"

"You will not harm my grandson," a man hissed in anger.

"Your grandson has become the monster. We must defend ourselves!"

The creature stomped on the floor and cracks spread across the wood from its hooves.

"It's trying to break through!"

"We have to get out of here," one of them choked out frantically. "If it breaks through, we'll all die."

"And where will we go? Just let that beast roam free while we hide in our homes?"

The wood of the door creaked and fell apart under Nightmare's antlers as it finally burst through, eyes gleaming in the light of the candles. It rose to stand on just two hooves within the taller space, looming over the villagers who had backed themselves as far from the area as possible.

"Run!" One of the men panicked and dropped his pitchfork as he scrambled away.

They broke out in separate directions, clambering around the furniture to escape through doors and windows. An elder was the last to go, staring at the monster with a sense of remorse, like a loss. Nightmare watched as they all ran away, their fear heavy on its tongue. It stared at the last villager, a hint of recognition from the vessel buried deep inside its hold. The old man didn't linger but instead hopped out of the window behind him. Taking slow steps forward, the creature's eyes crawled around the abandoned room. That same familiarity echoed from the mind trapped within the beast, and Nightmare concluded that this was the home of its latest iteration.

As it exited the house, it saw empty streets. Windows and doors were shut, lights had gone out, and silence hung thick in the air. But it could still hear the haggard breathing and hushed words of the villagers from where they hid. It could feel their trembling bodies as they huddled together, could feel their sense of apprehension, and their muscles wound tight.

A sense of movement caught its attention. A child stumbled out into the night, gasping for breath, and searched frantically for signs of danger. A memory of rocks being thrown flashed through the creature's mind. It got down on all fours again, measuring the distance to strike.

"Wilhelm! Where is Wilhelm?" a mother called out.

"Isn't he here?" the father replied in a rush.

They searched their home, every room, every closet, every cupboard, and any space to hide. Their son was missing.

A piercing cry chilled them, freezing them to the spot. They recognized the wail.

"Wilhelm!" the mother screamed. She burst out of the house before her husband could stop her.

There, in the dirt street of the cursed village, their son hung from Nightmare's points, impaled through the back with his face upturned to the sky. He was no longer wailing.

The mother collapsed to the ground, sobbing and reaching for the child as the father grabbed her. He held her close, weeping into her shoulder.

# 1630

## NEW MOON

The village was quiet, the sky gray. The wind moved autumn leaves through the dirt streets, but not a soul was in sight. A lone wanderer took slow steps forward, watching the buildings for signs of life. Something shifted in the old man's periphery, but when he turned, there was nothing, just a small house. He didn't realize his muscles were tense until he relaxed. Shuffling throughout the whole village, he knocked on doors and peered into windows to see only darkness. Thinking the place must be abandoned, the traveler headed back toward the path he came from.

Stumbling over something on the dirt road, he saw a dead squirrel at his feet. Curious, he slowly bent down to peer closer at the decaying rodent. His skin prickled and he turned to see a pair of reflective eyes staring at him through the bushes and thin trees of the forest. Startled, the man stood up so quickly that his joints popped. His breathing was haggard, legs tired and starting to shake. He leaned more heavily on his cane.

Whipping around toward the tree line, the eyes were gone but he still felt them on him. The weary wanderer scanned the village once more. His eyes kept going back to the tree line as the sun dipped down behind him. Shadows were cast onto the ground, and the wind picked up for a moment. There was something sour on the wind that pushed him toward the bushes. He kept going forward, brushing past branches, chasing after those eyes. As he went further into the woods the stench got harsher, like rotting carcasses left in the sun, causing him to hold a hand up to his nose. The air was stale, the grass brown and shriveled. The traveler bent down to touch the ground, digging his hands in to pick up a clod of dirt. There were worms and beetles, but they did not move. He picked a worm out, holding it in front of his face.

Beyond the limp worm, those eyes were staring back at him. The old man rose slowly, the eyes rising as well until they were level. They stared at each other for a moment, breaths coming out in a visible mist. The old man abruptly dropped the worm.

As a scream ripped through the air, the people inside the darkened houses of the nearby village shuddered as they sat huddled beneath windowsills and under tables. Some closed their eyes while others silently cried, clutching themselves and each other tightly.

"It's all for the good of the village," one whispered to himself. He was clutching a cross between his hands, eyes shut. "God, please forgive us, for we know not what we've done." He opened his eyes, raising his shaking hands in a pleading manner. "Please accept this sacrifice as atonement for our sins."

# 1632

## NEW MOON

"Retreat!" the call came out as the sun settled into the horizon. Soldiers scattered and hobbled away from the battlefield. The gunfire chased after them, making some flinch at the crack of flint and gunpowder. They rushed into the trees, fought against the brush, and narrowly avoided large trunks. As they raced toward safety, one soldier realized he'd been separated—they all had. Calls went out as they struggled to find each other. The trees blocked the sunlight, only small patches were bright enough.

Soon the yells were farther off, barely audible against the thick trees surrounding the soldier. He stumbled around in the direction he thought the latest shout had come from, only to hear another coming from a different direction. He glanced up at the leaves of the treetops, unable to tell if the sun was still up. There was only darkness. His hands reached out blindly, feeling for rough bark or soft leaves.

A scream pierced through the forest and the soldier's heart pounded loud in his ears. His harsh breathing broke the stark silence. He turned in every direction, searching frantically for the source. Another cry, not a call to rejoin or retreat, but a harkening of terror. It was cut off and the soldier shuddered. He sprinted faster as more shrieks surrounded him. They sounded like death throes, and he thought maybe the enemy had followed them in. He ran harder, scrambling through brush and tripping over roots.

His heartbeat nearly drowned out the hoofbeats from behind. Their horses had fled with them. The soldier, chest heaving, waited for one to arrive out of the darkness. His limbs ached from fighting and running. The hoofbeats were louder, almost upon him, and the air grew colder. He dug through his kit until he found a lantern and yanked it out, struggling to light it. He knelt down and held the lantern in front of him to witness the green foliage wither to brown—along with hooves stamping down upon them.

He rose up quickly as a squealing horse barreled through the trees straight at him, nearly knocking him over. He jumped out of the way, watching as the mare stumbled through the clearing. The bushes rustled behind him. He turned and met face-to-face with what had frightened the warhorse. His shriek died with him.

# 10

# The Last Goodbye

## WANING CRESCENT MOON

## 1636

**W**endell woke with his heart racing and breath heaving. He sat up quickly, eyes searching his surroundings wildly. He was in his room, on the floor with some blankets. Next to him, Jacques was sleeping in his bed, his chest rising and falling steadily. With a relieved exhale, Wendell's breathing began to calm down and his heart slowed. He went to lie back down when he heard shuffling coming from nearby. Curious, he stood up and peeked out of the doorway. He saw a light coming from down the hall. Wendell glanced back at Jacques before stepping out of his room. He tapped on the door where the light was coming from and the shuffling stopped, then the door opened to reveal his grandfather.

The man's face was older, his skin sagging with wrinkles and his beard completely gray. He was dressed like he was going out into town. "Grandfather, what are you . . ." Wendell began to ask before noticing an old, dirty travel bag on the floor, still open with supplies tucked neatly inside. Wendell gazed back at his grandfather, who was giving him a sad smile.

"I think it's time, Wendell."

Wendell shook his head. "You can't leave, not yet, Jacques is still—"

His grandfather interrupted him. "Healing well, and the two of you are growing close. While I still can, I want to find the answers to this curse."

"While you still can?" Wendell asked. He didn't want to think of what his grandfather was trying to tell him—the signs of aging, the slower gait—all pointed to an imminent demise.

The older man gestured to his appearance. "Being in Nightmare's presence has aged me, and I fear the process is quickening. I may not have much time left before I succumb to the curse myself."

"But Jacques survived, so that means you can as well!" Wendell exclaimed. It had to; he couldn't bear the thought of losing his grandfather so soon after his parents. He didn't know what he would do if he were left alone in this world.

The other shook his head slowly. "No, Wendell. Jacques is special. He must be. That is why I must go on one last journey to find the truth."

Lowering his head, Wendell murmured, "I wish I could go with you." He had always wished he could leave this village and go on the adventures his grandfather often told him about. He yearned for an escape from a life of avoidance and guilt.

"You must stay here and continue caring for Jacques. He will protect you in return. Katharina and Obstein are on your side. You are not alone, Wendell." His grandfather reached out and ruffled his hair fondly. Wendell had felt the distance growing between them, and now it was like his grandfather was already so far away. Tears started falling down his cheeks.

"I must go into town to gather more supplies. Would you like to go with me?" his grandfather asked. Wendell nodded, wiping his tears. He ran to his room to get dressed and wash his face before rejoining his grandfather outside.

The townspeople glared at them as they passed but were paid no heed. They entered the mapmaker's shop to find the cartographer bending over his latest map. He stood up to see them and blinked in surprise.

"Ah, Albrecht. What brings you here?"

"I need a new map and some supplies."

The cartographer raised his eyebrows, briefly glancing at Wendell. "Planning to leave?" He leaned his elbow on the counter.

The elder's face hardened. "I'm going to find answers, Martin. The curse won't spread as long as Wendell is alive."

The mapmaker, wary, didn't question him any further. Instead, he turned to the wall of shelving behind him. "I have a few maps that are the most up-to-date, or would you prefer something older?"

"I just need something to point me in the right direction."

When they returned from gathering the supplies needed for his journey, Wendell's grandfather placed them inside his travel bag. It reeked of stale cheese and was still caked in dried mud. Dust from the cracked, muddy residue flew into the air as he set the sack on his workbench.

"Why didn't you get a new one?" Wendell asked, nose scrunched up from the stench and debris coming from the worn bag.

"This one has lasted me several journeys," his grandfather replied. "I want to take it with me on my last one. It holds memories I do not wish to forget." He began loading the bag with supplies new and old—tucking extra clothing in amongst sturdy, slightly dented dishes, then wrapping a newly purchased compass in a cloth and placing it next to a metal canteen.

"Your grandmother and I used to travel a lot, when we first got married," he explained. "A seasoned traveler never forgets the essentials." He winked at Wendell, who gave a tentative smile in return.

"Jacques, I must ask you something."

The old man came to him at night. Wendell was already asleep when Albrecht requested Jacques to join him in the living area. They sat in worn chairs with only a dim light in the room.

"I am leaving the village tomorrow morning to search for answers," Albrecht told him.

"What about Wendell?" Jacques asked.

"Please protect him in my absence," Albrecht whispered.

Jacques knew he would defend the other no matter what—Wendell was a kind soul in a cruel world. He deserved someone to stand by his side against it all. "From the villagers, or himself?" he asked with a wry smile.

Albrecht gave a soft chuckle. "So, you know." He sat back with a sigh of relief. "The villagers are still afraid of Nightmare's wrath, so they are not likely to hurt him. They may get fussy occasionally, but you simply need to remind them of their sins of the past and they will eventually settle down."

"Sins of the past?" Jacques asked him.

Albrecht grimaced. "There was a time when the people here thought that killing the babies born under a new moon would stop the curse, but that only served to end family lines. Then came a terrible plague during the harvest that destroyed our crops. Many lost their livestock to a sickness that spread from farm to farm. We consulted with the Church and agreed to let the cursed ones live instead of letting everyone suffer. We still had to endure sacrifices, but they were less damaging than whole generations lost to time."

Jacques nodded in understanding. He leaned forward to hear more of the old man's wisdom. "But my grandson takes the curse upon himself like a burden only he can bear. I've helped him carry the weight, but he must learn to carry it on his own. You understand what I mean, yes?"

"Yes," Jacques replied. "And I think Wendell is strong enough to carry it; he just doesn't know it yet."

This time Albrecht smiled at him. "You must make him know."

It was a cold, gray day when Wendell's grandfather departed. He had his traveling cloak on, and the dirt-encrusted bag filled with supplies slung around his shoulder.

Wendell waited for him outside of his door, face pale. "Do you really have to go?" he asked softly.

"Yes, I must," the old man told him, taking a step forward. "For your sake, I need to find answers."

Wendell moved out of the way, allowing the elder to pass. "But what about . . ." he began, trailing off. He stared at the wood floors, lacing and unlacing his fingers. His grandfather waited for him to continue. "What if the villagers try to stop you?" Wendell finally asked, eyes piercing through him.

"They can try," the old man replied. His face crinkled as he smiled. "Don't worry about them, you have Jacques with you now. He will protect you."

Despite the tears welling in Wendell's eyes, the boy smiled back at him. "May God guide you on your journey, Grandfather."

"You remind me so much of your mother, Wendell," his grandfather said suddenly. He reached out and lay a hand on Wendell's head. "She was kind, like you are, and always thought of others before herself. The curse changed her. This village changed her. Don't let it change you, too."

Wendell, unable to utter words, bowed his head.

His grandfather turned to his workstation, which was tidy and clean; not a wood shaving to be seen. He picked up a clock with ornate details carved around the edges and handed it to Wendell, who reached for it.

Wendell's eyes focused on the top carving, where a buck's head with tall antlers emerged from the leaves. His grandfather watched as he accepted the gift, his eyes shining with tears and throat working to swallow around a lump.

"I made this for you; I wanted my last one to be special. It is the only thing I can leave behind for you," the clockmaker said, voice tight with emotion as if he were trying to hold back tears of his own.

"Thank you," Wendell said, lifting his head. He clutched the clock to his chest.

For what was possibly the last time, his grandfather leaned in to kiss his forehead. "Goodbye, Wendell."

"Goodbye, Grandfather."

# 11

# The Earnest Promise

## NEW MOON

**A**s the days passed by, Jacques felt himself getting back to normal. He tested the strength of his arm, performing exercises Doctor Obstein showed him to help with the healing process. Once he was able to move around on his own, he helped Wendell with tasks around the house—without the presence of Wendell's grandfather and parents, it seemed large and lonely.

Jacques caught himself watching Wendell and saw overwhelming sorrow and guilt in those large, cervine eyes. He thought about broaching the subject with him but could never get the words past his lips. Instead, they sat on the porch steps and silently watched the village. Sometimes Jacques went for a walk around the town, just to get out of the foreboding home.

On one such walk, he wandered into the baker's shop. The sweet smell of fresh bread and cakes filled the air, making his mouth water. Humming to himself, he perused the delicacies, trying to decide which one to bring back home.

"You, traveler," the baker's voice startled Jacques as the man rounded the corner. "Come to steal more?"

"Oh, no sir. I apologize, I was in a rush and not thinking properly that morning," Jacques replied quickly.

The baker raked his eyes over him. "The name is Bäcker."

Jacques ducked his head. "Mine is Jacques."

"You should have never come back, Jacques," Bäcker stated gruffly. "Maybe they'd still be alive."

Jacques frowned, feeling his limbs tense up under the fierce expression from the other man. "Who, sir?" he asked politely.

"Marla and Hansel," the baker replied. "They only died because you escaped the curse."

Stepping back, Jacques blinked furiously, unsure of how to respond. He opened his mouth, but only stuttered sounds came out.

Bäcker shook his head, going to a counter to knead some powdered dough. He spoke as his fists molded the substance. "It should have been one of Harold's cows, or old man Beecher. He's lived a good enough life."

"I'm sorry," Jacques said, although he was unsure whether he was apologizing for the death of Wendell's parents or his own lack of understanding.

Bäcker paused in his work. "They were good people. Honest, hard-working, caring people. Until *he* was born." He spat the last part out like tough meat.

Jacques recoiled, feeling anger boil up. "Wendell is a good person, too," he said vehemently. "His parents did not seem to be too caring when I was in their company. They were the ones who compelled me to leave when I did."

"Don't talk to me as if you know any of them, boy," Bäcker snarled. "You are new to this place; you haven't endured what we have for generations. You don't fear the night the same way we do."

Jacques clenched his jaw, keeping his mouth shut for fear of stirring up a frenzy. He exhaled. "You're right, I don't. But have any of you ever stopped to think about how *he* feels? How difficult it must be to bear this curse on your shoulders without asking?"

Bäcker frowned at him harshly and picked up a round, long tool. Jacques prepared himself for an attack, but none came. The baker rolled the tool back and forth over the dough, squishing it into place under the weight. "We know," he said in a low tone. "But it doesn't make it right."

Despite Bäcker's grouchy demeanor, Jacques came home with baked goods. He found Wendell standing in the doorway of his grandfather's room, staring at the table where Albrecht made his clocks.

"I brought some food, if you want it," Jacques told him softly.

Wendell sniffed the air. "I smell berries," he remarked, turning to Jacques. "And sugar."

Jacques grinned. "Wow, you have a good nose."

Wendell shrugged. "The curse gives each person special traits," he clarified as he took the wrapped treats from Jacques and entered the kitchen, setting them on the counter to grab plates from the cupboards.

"I would have bought some meat as well, but . . ." Jacques tapered off, rubbing the back of his neck. He still had little money to buy goods.

Wendell stared at the empty food storage. "Father used to get pork from the butcher. Sometimes lamb, too." He placed his hands on the counter, staring down at them. "The family raised cattle to slaughter. They would sell most of it to the village but keep some for us." He paused. "But one month, the herd was struck with a disease that spread even to the calves, and they lost most of them. No one would buy meat from the ones that survived, so they had to sell them off to the next merchants who came to town."

"Was it . . . the curse?" Jacques asked. At Wendell's surprised expression, he added, "Your grandfather told me about generations of families being lost and plagues killing livestock if there were no sacrifices made."

Wendell's eyes widened briefly. "Yes," he said sadly. Focusing on his hands, he added, "most of the village believes it is better to lose one life than allow everyone to suffer."

Silence overtook them as they prepared a small meal from the bread, cheeses, and fruits they had left over. Albrecht had ensured enough food to last them a few days after he left, taking some for his own travels to avoid too much spoilage, but they were already low. The money left from Wendell's parents and grandfather was safely kept away to use for house repairs and emergencies, but even that would not last much longer. With Wendell shunned and unable to work, it was up to Jacques to take care of the person who had nursed him back to health.

Jacques swallowed. "I will find some meat for us," he said. He took a step closer to Wendell. "I won't let you starve. I promised your grandfather to keep you safe. I'm going to uphold that promise." His voice was steady, and his eyes determined as he stared at Wendell.

As the sky darkened outside, Jacques felt the air tighten all around him. He wondered briefly why his muscles were tense and his throat aching. The wounds in his arms and stomach pulsed, reminding him of a similar night.

Wendell appeared in front of the door, giving Jacques a fright as he did not hear his footsteps enter the room. "Is it . . ." he began to ask.

Wendell's hair bobbed as he nodded. "A new moon is out," he

said in a faint voice. "The village locks down as soon as the sun sets."
He finally turned to Jacques. "Stay inside."

Jacques did not need to be told why. He would rather not encounter Nightmare again. The memory of pain still lingered, enough to plague his dreams and torment his waking thoughts. "So, you go out there every time?" Jacques dared to ask.

"Yes," Wendell answered. He stiffened, yet stood casually, his head tilted as if listening for something. Jacques knew he could hear things others could not, but he wasn't sure what sound he was expecting.

"All alone?" Jacques asked quietly. The thought of the young man venturing out into the darkness of the woods where horrors beyond measure awaited turned his stomach. What if a predator caught him?

Wendell sounded wistful as he responded. "When I was younger, Grandfather would walk with me to the edge of the tree line and then come find me in the morning. No one else wanted to be out during that time."

It struck Jacques that his worries were for naught. He was staring at the predator, the thing the night feared, not some weak farm boy. For the first time, he felt afraid of Wendell, but when he thought of the young man's smile and gentle words, he shoved the fear aside. Nightmare was the thing to be scared of, not Wendell.

Turning back to him, Wendell said, "I can make it back here on my own. You don't have to wait up for me." And then he slipped out of the door, disappearing down the trail into the forest lit only by the stars overhead.

Despite his words, Jacques couldn't sleep or move from his spot on the chair, curled up on himself. Memories of the snow-covered forest, antlers stained with blood, and Albrecht's pleading form flashed within his mind. He couldn't get the image of the bony, matted fur and grotesque maw of the beast out of his head. The stench of rotting meat and something sour was stuck in his nostrils. He held his linen shirt up to his nose and breathed in deep, trying to replace it with the smell of wood and fresh flowers—the smell of the house, of Wendell. Every time he closed his eyes, he saw the decomposing fawn and its half-eaten mother.

His eyes were tired and burning by the time dawn approached, but still he stayed awake. He worried that this time Wendell wouldn't come back. Panic kept his head from slipping down to rest against the windowsill. He couldn't live with himself if he failed to keep his promise to Wendell's grandfather. The thought of the villagers with pitchforks and fires surrounding Wendell deep in the woods made his heart pound. He was about to get up and search. A figure emerged from the trees. Staring, the familiar way in which the person walked and how the sun lit up their pale hair assured him it was his friend coming back home. Slowly unfurling himself, he stood up to open the door as Wendell mounted the steps. His clothes were dirty and rumpled, ripped in places, but what stood out most was the splatters of blood on his fair face.

Wendell, surprised to see him, paused on the porch. "You waited," he said in a hoarse voice.

Jacques ignored the blood as he embraced Wendell, arms wrapping tightly around his shoulders. "I waited," he whispered.

## WAXING CRESCENT

Jacques asked around town about work, and eventually, the innkeeper let him on as a hand in the tavern when things got too busy for him and his wife to handle. The money was just enough to feed the two and pay their dues to the lord of the land.

"I wish there was a way to help," Wendell sighed. "I feel like a burden to you like I was to my family."

"You're no burden, Wendy," Jacques reassured him. "Say, what did they do for work? I know your grandfather was a clockmaker, but what about your parents?"

"After the family livestock was sold, my father turned the farm into cropland," Wendell replied. "But he never taught me. Mother would help." His gaze went out of the window into the fields where seeds had been sown into the ground in lines earlier that year. "I watched them plant the seeds and water them to see if I could learn—and when harvest time came, I offered to help bring some to the town market, but I was never allowed in the fields. Father thought my presence would ruin the soil."

Jacques frowned at him as he spoke. "I may be able to help come harvest time. What has been planted?"

Wendell scrunched up his face for a moment as he recalled what his father had sown. "I believe it was wheat."

Jacques nodded. "Then come summer, I will help you collect and sell whatever the land yields." He turned to Wendell, who started to smile at him until the corners of his mouth nearly reached his eyes. He looked happy and hopeful for the first time in a long while. Jacques smiled at him in return.

"Have you heard about the witch trials?" Jacques asked Wendell the next day over dinner.

Wendell shook his head, biting into his bread. "Only the war. What are the trials?"

"They're burning people at the stake now. I read it in a newspaper." Jacques frowned. "There are people who call themselves witch hunters who find people accused of witchcraft and put them on trial. I didn't believe in that kind of thing until I got to this place."

Wendell paused in his meal. "Some of the villagers think the curse was caused by witchcraft many generations ago, but the original witch was unknown. They claim people like me are 'descendants' even though our family lines are not always the same," he said.

"I suppose it would be easy for them to believe," Jacques suggested. "Especially with how much the Church has sought to squash it out." He snorted in disdain at the thought.

"Do you think a witch hunter will come here one day?" Wendell's hands shook and his voice wavered. "The village has tried nearly everything to get rid of the curse. They used to kill anyone who displayed the signs." He brought his gaze up at Jacques. "Like my eyes. They're the mark of the deer. Loxley's teeth were said to be pointed and sharp like a wolf."

Jacques recoiled at the description. "I like your eyes better than I would his teeth."

Wendell laughed before he could stop himself, covering his mouth with a hand. Jacques grinned at him from across the table.

"Well, if any witch hunter comes into town, I vow to keep you safe," Jacques told him earnestly. Wendell's face grew red, and he blinked. Jacques felt his own cheeks burning and fought the urge to glance away. "I mean it, Wendell. I will not let anyone hurt you."

"But why?" Wendell whispered. "After what I did to you . . ." he trailed off, pointedly focusing on Jacques' bandaged arm.

Jacques shook his head. "You did not hurt me, Wendell. You were the one who stayed by my side and helped me heal."

Wendell ducked his head bashfully. "How do you know about that?" he mumbled.

"Your grandfather told me. He said you were there day and night, applying the herbs Katharina brought and cleaning my wounds. He would often find you asleep after tending to me and said you only left my side to eat and bathe. I truly appreciate all you have done for me, Wendell."

"It was the least I could do. I couldn't watch you die," Wendell replied in a small voice.

Jacques reached across the table and took Wendell's hand in his own. "Thank you for not giving up on me." He stared into those odd yet beautiful eyes until he was sure Wendell understood.

"Not many people are this kind to me. Only Grandfather," Wendell said. "My parents weren't happy when I was born."

"You cannot help how or when you are born." Jacques squeezed Wendell's hand for emphasis.

"The people here don't think so. Even with the lunar calendar, it can be hard to predict when a child will come. That's why not many children are here—no one wants to bear a curse."

"I was wondering about that," Jacques said.

"People have even tried to leave, but others feared that the curse would spread. Grandfather talked with the lord of our land and a law was made that no one can leave once they've planted their roots here. I was worried they wouldn't let Grandfather go, but since he's already endured the curse . . ."

"They weren't worried that he'd carry it with him," Jacques finished for him. Wendell nodded. "So, travelers can come and go as they please, then?"

Something changed in Wendell's face, briefly, but Jacques could not identify it. "We rely on scholars and merchants passing through for knowledge and goods to trade, so yes." Wendell contemplated something, worrying his mouth. "Once you are fully healed, I suppose you could leave to continue your travels," he mumbled.

"No," Jacques said, surprising Wendell. "I plan to stay right here."

"But what about your journey?" Wendell asked. "Are you not afraid of Nightmare?"

Jacques winced at the mention of the beast but grinned at Wendell's bewildered expression. "I have traveled for some time now—I should stay here for a while. I don't mind. You are nice company to have."

Wendell's face reddened again, and he stared down at their entwined fingers, then glanced back up shyly from beneath his bangs. "I would like it if you stayed. I enjoy your company as well."

"Tell me about where you're from," Wendell said as they relaxed on the front porch. The sky was clear and the air crisp, making it a fine day to sit outside. Jacques was leaning back on his hands, his legs kicked up on the stairs. Wendell sat next to him at the top of the steps with his arms over his knees.

Jacques tensed up a bit. "Ah, a small place, just across the Rhine," he answered.

Wendell turned his head toward him. "What is it like there?" His curiosity was innocent and benign, but Jacques could not help feeling as though he were being pressed for answers. He did not believe Wendell had any ill intentions, but he hesitated in responding.

"Well, it certainly is nothing like this." He laughed it off, tossing his head back toward the sky.

"I have only read about places outside of here," Wendell told him. "I once dreamed of being able to travel the world and see all the things described in the books and scrolls kept in the town hall's library. Grandfather would sometimes tell me about where he went with Grandmother when they were younger."

Jacques exhaled. "Would you like me to tell you about my travels, and the places I've seen?" He relaxed when Wendell nodded, smiling. "Although not always the most pleasant experience, I enjoyed being on the road on days like this. When I could not find an inn to stay at, I would sleep on the ground, under the stars. They are so beautiful, and I was learning the constellations from a map." Wendell was listening in rapt attention. "But sometimes I would have to wash up in a river, and the water was always icy cold!" He wrapped his arms around himself to demonstrate the chill and Wendell laughed. The rest of the evening was spent that way—with Jacques telling Wendell about his journey from his hometown to how he ended up in the village, until the sky was dark and full of bright stars.

# 12

# The Dreaded Arrival

## FIRST QUARTER MOON

**There was a stir in** the village one morning. Wendell felt a vibration in the air that tightened his stomach. He stepped out onto the porch and picked up an unfamiliar scent in the wind. The cause of the smell came riding in on four horses. They were clothed like travelers, but there were no wagons with them containing wares; nor had they the appearance of scholars, but instead like they came from the Church. All appeared to be foreigners, though Wendell could hardly place where each one came from.

Villagers were peeking out of their doors and windows to take in the strangers. The group rode past Wendell's home, giving him barely a glance as they headed toward the center of town. A trail of curious inhabitants followed them at a distance. Whispers filled the air, with one word being repeated enough to make Wendell shiver.

"They're Inquisitors."

Wendell startled, turning to find Jacques at his side, squinting after the group with a frown. "Inquisitors?" he asked.

"Those witch hunters I was telling you about, the Church has started granting them special permission to arrest and try witches. They're called Inquisitors." Jacques replied in a hard tone.

"How can you tell who they are?" Wendell said, even though he had a feeling Jacques was right.

"I've seen them depicted in notices before—their garments are similar. I can't believe they found this place." Jacques' jaw was clenched. Wendell could feel anger coming off him in static waves. He turned his harsh gaze from the group to Wendell, eyes softening. "I meant what I said. If they come after you, I'll stop them."

Wendell swallowed and took a shallow breath. The air had the same taste as on a new moon. It crackled, threatening to spark into a raging flame around them. It made Wendell feel cold, and he wrapped his arms around himself instinctually. He took a step back, then turned quickly to go inside.

Jacques followed the crowd into the village, wanting to hear for himself what they planned to do here. He stood along the outer edge, listening in.

Stuber stood outside of his inn, observing the strangers warily. "Are you travelers in need of lodgings?"

"Yes," one of the Inquisitors responded in English, dismounting from his horse. He stood a foot taller than the innkeeper and had striking blond hair cut short to his ears. Jacques was surprised to hear English this deep within the Empire, recognizing a few words and phrases from his travels. The others remained on their horses, imposing and different. One of them, a woman with curly brown hair and a round face, leaned over their stallion to get a better glimpse at a nearby totem. Another was surveying the gathered villagers with narrowed eyes. Their horses snorted and shifted from hoof to hoof.

Stuber gestured behind him. "We have a fine place for you to stay and plenty of food to fill your bellies." He told the tall blond man. Jacques frowned at his tone of voice. It was friendly and welcoming, unlike the hostility displayed when Jacques had asked for a room.

"I appreciate your hospitality," the other man responded in the same language, though with a distinctly different dialect. He glanced around the village, giving a slight nod to himself. "We've arrived just in time," he added in English. Stuber's wide smile faltered as he parsed out the meaning of the stranger's words.

The Inquisitor who had been straining to see the totems rummaged through a bag tied to the side of the horse, pulling out a well-used scroll. She pointed at it and spoke cheerfully with a different accent than the blond, although Jacques could not fully understand what she said. He recognized the lunar charts her finger indicated, however, and felt his stomach drop. He moved closer to the innkeeper in order to hear and see better.

Bäcker turned to Stuber and whispered, "What are they saying?" Stuber shrugged, gesturing to the scroll the Englishwoman held. "You don't think they mean . . ." he said in a hushed voice.

"That's impossible," Fleischer responded sharply, staring at the newcomers with furrowed brows. "They can't know." Others in the crowd began to murmur, gathering closer.

The tall man smiled at Stuber and said in their language, "We hear you have a problem with witchcraft in this town. Perhaps we can help."

Curious now, Bäcker said, "And where did you hear that?"

"Tales have spread to the Church about strange deaths and plagues in this area. Are they true?" he asked.

The villagers whispered furiously to themselves, turning to each other frantically. Jacques could feel his pulse speed up and took a step back. *They know about the curse.*

"So, you are Inquisitors!" Fleischer exclaimed. "Come to hunt down the witch that has cursed us, eh?"

"Lord, have mercy," a woman gasped, leaning against another and clasping her hand to her chest.

The stranger held up a hand. "Excuse me, I've yet to introduce us. My name is Irving, and we are indeed Inquisitors of the Pope. Please do not be alarmed by our presence."

The villagers appeared to consider this, and Jacques knew Wendell was in trouble. He saw the crowd part as the priest appeared. "I welcome you in the name of Our Lord," he greeted. "I am Father Heinrich. Please come with me, and we shall discuss the matter." He held out his arm, gesturing for them to follow. Irving turned to the other three and gave a nod. They dismounted and tied their horses to the tack outside of the inn. One of them was almost identical to Irving, with longer hair and a beard—likely a relative. His face was hard, and the crowd hurriedly stepped out of his way. The woman who had spoken earlier carried a black bag that resembled the one Doctor Obstein and Katharina brought with them when Jacques was recovering. The third was shorter than the rest, with long black wavy hair and a goatee. His eyes were piercing, drifting carefully over the villagers as if waiting for something to happen.

Jacques snuck around the outskirts of the gathering to watch them head toward the church. Feeling desperate, he headed toward the apothecary to seek Obstein's advice. After a few knocks on the door, Katharina answered. "Hello dear," she greeted. When she saw his expression, she added, "Is there something wrong? Are you feeling well?"

"Inquisitors have come," he said in a rush. Panicking, he continued, "I think they're here for the curse—for Wendell. Is there anything to be done?"

The midwife startled, peering out of the door to see the lingering crowd still discussing the presence of the strangers. She pulled

Jacques in gently, leading him through the apothecary to the back where Obstein sat at his desk, viewing his notes. At the sound of their footsteps, his head lifted from the documents to regard them.

"Ah, is there some emergency?" Obstein asked.

"Doctor, we have visitors," Katharina told him in a serious tone. She gestured to Jacques.

"Inquisitors have just arrived." He explained. "The priest is meeting with them now at the church."

Obstein swept his gaze from one to the other, unconcerned. "And? What has this to do with me?"

"I'm worried they're here because of Nightmare. Wendell could be in danger!" Jacques exclaimed.

The doctor took off his glasses and set them down on his desk. Jacques saw that the notes were about his injuries and recovery. Obstein piled them together and set them aside carefully. "I see," he said in a reserved tone. "You are his guardian now, yes?"

Jacques nodded at him, feeling his heart speed up. "Will you help us?"

Obstein folded his hands together. "I will do what I can, out of respect for the Uhrmacher family. I cannot guarantee his safety, however, should they choose to condemn him."

Jacques felt his anger rising. "Why not?"

"I am only a man, Jacques," Obstein said softly. "I cannot stand between the church and their judgment."

There was a knock on the door. The three of them turned, Jacques breathing in quickly. Katharina peered through the curtains. "It's them, with Father Heinrich," she whispered.

Obstein gestured at Jacques, "Hide yourself. I will handle this." Jacques nodded and ducked into the closest door nearby, a medicine closet. He peered through a crack as Katharina went to open the door. He could barely make out what they said, and soon footsteps indicated they were coming down the hall.

"Doctor, I request your assistance," Jacques heard the priest say. "These people have come a long way seeking answers." The way he locked eyes with Obstein made Jacques feel unsettled. He got a closer look at the group of travelers, recognizing flecks of dried blood that had not completely washed out on one's shirt. He angled his head to see which one it was but could only glimpse part of the shirt through the limited viewpoint of the closet door's small opening.

"Welcome," Obstein said as he rose from his desk. "Is it some disease? I'm hardly the most qualified."

"No, Doctor," Father Heinrich told him. He gestured behind him. "They're Inquisitors, and they've come to our aid concerning the curse set upon us by God." He gave the doctor a knowing expression.

Jacques frowned. He thought of Albrecht, who had been gone for quite some time now, and of Wendell sobbing by his side as he was healing from the wounds inflicted by Nightmare. Wendell was not the one to blame for what had happened—he kept his vow to protect him from anything that would hurt him.

Putting his hands behind his back, Obstein took on a scholarly manner. "I have been searching for a cure for a long time, Father. Unless they are here to help in that regard, I do not think they are needed."

The clergyman's face pinked. "With all due respect, Obstein, I believe we have suffered under this affliction long enough, and they are offering their services to us."

"Actually," one of the Inquisitors spoke up—the Englishwoman. Irving translated for her. "I'm interested in your research, Doctor." She stepped forward and dropped her bag on his desk, opened it, and began digging through it. Jacques was able to see her fully. Her shirt was the one with blood stains. Taking out vials and scrolls, the woman added, "You see, I've done quite a bit of research myself on such things. We just need a little more information on what kind of witchcraft this is and how the curse came to be." She stuck out her hand to him. "The name is Anna."

Obstein regarded her with interest and surprise, shaking her hand slowly. Jacques watched as he picked up one of the vials and glanced back up at her. Anna remained smiling at him, a much different demeanor than the men who stood behind her.

Irving stepped up beside her. "Apologies for the intrusion, Doctor," he said kindly and introduced himself. "Our mission is to help people such as yourself and the rest of this town who are afflicted with supernatural phenomena. As Anna said, we would like more information about this curse so we can determine how best to overcome it."

Jacques measured the crinkle of Irving's eyes and his charming smile. Obstein glanced at the other two, the one who appeared related to Irving and the one who had an edge to his expression. "Very well," he said. Jacques listened as the doctor and Katharina gave the Inquisitors a brief history of the cursed town, watching how the strangers reacted.

"Exorcisms, executions, the elimination of entire bloodlines . . . you've certainly tried everything, it seems," Anna murmured.

"Sacrifices have been made, some regrettable, in the pursuit of a cure," Obstein remarked solemnly.

Father Heinrich added quickly, "At first we believed it was a demon, possessing villagers to punish us."

Irving gave him a sympathetic smile. "I understand why you would come to such a conclusion. Demons are a dangerous business."

"But this is no demon," Anna said, tucking loose strands of hair behind her ear as she peered over documents Obstein has produced. "That much is obvious, even with what little information you have."

"What she means is that a man of the cloth like yourself would surely be able to dispel such a creature if it were," Irving said at the affronted expression on Father Heinrich's face.

"Yes, well, we've realized that now," the priest spluttered.

"Not a demon, nor a disease," Obstein stated. "At this point, I've come to think of it as a parasite."

Anna beamed at the doctor. "Yes, I agree. It seems more parasitic in nature than anything else. The fact that it attaches itself to newborns of this village, regardless of relation to the villagers, makes it more than a mere shapeshifter."

"A shapeshifter?" Katharina asked. Jacques furrowed his eyebrows, just as confused as the midwife sounded.

"People who can change shape and turn into something else," Irving replied.

Father Heinrich paled. "Those beings are among us?"

"Closer than you think," the shorter man snorted with a heavy accent, different from Irving's. Irving glanced at him with a stern expression, and the Inquisitor returned to inspecting Obstein's workspace.

"Yes, Anna is referring to a type of being that can transform. Usually this occurs to people within a certain relation or is transferred from one to another through various means; but from your observations, this does not appear to be the case," Irving explained.

Obstein's eyebrows came together, and he put a hand to his chin. "I'd like to hear more of your reasoning to reject such a theory; not that I disagree, but I have not heard of such a being before."

Anna answered. "In relation to bloodlines, you disproved that by killing several newborns a few generations ago—"

"That was an attempt to dispel the curse. It was a terrible time, but we felt it had to be done," Father Heinrich interrupted. He was sweating and fidgeting nervously.

Anna blinked at him, offering a slight nod before continuing, "As for the other methods, you would have likely observed wounds from bites or scratches, almost like an attack from a large animal."

Obstein nodded in understanding. "The victims of Nightmare have such wounds, but all die immediately," he said.

"Do any of them revive?" Anna asked. The clergyman was flustered and appalled at her question.

Katharina replied to her in a soft tone. "No, madam, they remain buried."

"And it can affect anyone within the village?" Anna asked her.

"Yes, those who settle here are bound to be cursed eventually," Katharina said.

"That's something I'd like to discuss," Irving said, adopting a more serious manner. "As far as this curse spreading, I fear it would be detrimental to all humanity."

Father Heinrich waved his hand dismissively. "No need to worry. The curse stays in this village. It hasn't affected anywhere else."

"You're wrong, Father," Luis spoke again. "Clear tracks of decay surround this village, and other townships close by have been forced to go elsewhere for the resources they need due to bad soil. It's only a matter of time before it manifests in nearby cities." Jacques remembered seeing signs of rot as he wandered through the forest and ran into the dead fawn. The snow on the ground covered up most of the damage, but he had witnessed the effect on the buildings and nearby trees.

The priest, midwife, and doctor exchanged glances. Father Heinrich made the sign of the cross over himself and Obstein sighed, folding his arms. "That is precisely what we have feared," he said. "Nightmare poisons the Earth wherever it treads; we have already lost fields of crops and livestock over several generations from the curse's impact. We found ways to live with it, but we have always tried to prevent it from affecting other villages or towns."

"Are you referring to your practice of luring innocent travelers in to use as sacrifices?" the short man stated plainly, though his tone denounced judgment.

"Luis," Irving hissed, attempting to silence him.

Luis brushed him off, coming closer. "Your warning signs are well placed, but not effective. There have been multiple stories of people wandering into this area and never coming out. Judging by your population, I do not assume those wanderers now live here."

"Where did you get such folly from?" Father Heinrich whispered furiously.

The Inquisitors changed their stances from casual to stiff. Jacques already had an idea of where they had come across such information. Only one person was as passionate about finding a way to free the people of this town from the curse as they sounded, and he had left long enough to have met them on the road if they were already traveling this way.

"We met someone from this village who told us most of what we know," Irving said, confirming Jacques' thoughts. "He begged us to come here and lend our aid."

The doctor and the clergyman studied each other, their eyes alight with knowledge. Jacques let out a gasp before covering his mouth. He glanced at the group, who remained watching Obstein and Father Heinrich. Except for Anna, who stared right at him with a friendly smile. Jacques shifted back, away from the door, fearful that he would be discovered.

"I see," Obstein said and sighed. "You have given me much to think about. Allow me some time to gather more information to share with you. I have appointments I need to attend this evening."

"Of course, we'll come back tomorrow to discuss matters further," Irving said. He extended his hand to the doctor. "Thank you for speaking with us, Doctor. I look forward to working with you further on this." Obstein shook his hand and nodded. Father Heinrich grasped his shoulder tightly and then followed the group out of the apothecary.

As soon as they were gone, Jacques rushed back to Wendell's house as fast as he could, wincing at the ache in his stomach and wheezing by the time he got there. Breathless, he told Wendell what he heard.

Wendell paced up and down the hall, wringing his hands and gnawing at his lip. Jacques was leaning against the wall, watching him.

"You don't have to worry," Jacques said calmly. Wendell heard the anxiousness in his voice despite the attempt to hide it. "I won't let them near you."

"It's not me I'm worried about," Wendell said. Jacques' eyebrows came together. "One of them may become the sacrifice if they stay here too long."

Jacques softened his expression. "They've come to kill you, and you're more concerned about their fate than your own."

Wendell stopped, his hands stilling. "What if they're not here to kill me?" His eyes locked onto Jacques.

Jacques shook his head. "Before I came to this village, I thought the witch hunters were mad for chasing after ghost stories. Now that I know about the curse, it's more likely they've come to accuse you of witchcraft like they do all the others."

Wendell stepped closer to him. "But if they can find a cure—" he began.

"Inquisitors are never interested in a cure," Jacques spat. "They're only interested in the bounty for their services." Wendell recoiled from him, and Jacques reached out. "I'm sorry," he said in a milder tone. "I've just heard some terrible things about them." He felt terrified for Wendell after hearing what became of people accused of being witches. Torture and gruesome deaths always followed in the wake of Inquisitors of the Church.

Wendell's large, unnatural eyes stared at him. "You heard terrible things about me as well; yet you remain by my side."

Jacques pursed his lips. "You're different," he said.

"They could be different, too," Wendell pointed out.

"Or just like the rest: bloodthirsty and greedy. Think about it, Wendell; how could they have heard about you—about the curse? The only people who know are from this village." He sighed and closed his eyes, dragging a hand through his hair. "Anyway, I just don't think we can trust them. Not yet at least."

"Maybe one of them asked the Church…" Jacques saw Wendell's expression change, eyes wide and mouth slightly open. "From the village," Wendell repeated to himself, staring off into the distance. "Grandfather," he breathed in a revelation. Turning back to Jacques, he asked, "What if he sent them to help?"

Jacques wanted to feel that same sense of optimism and faith that he saw in Wendell's face, but a sinking feeling weighed him down. He had the same thought earlier while he was hiding in the apothecary, but something didn't feel right. "Where is he then? Would he not have come back with them?" He winced at the fallen expression on the other's face.

Wendell pressed on. "He might still be searching for more answers in case they can't help." Hope was strong in his face and voice. Jacques could not bear to see it broken. Instead, he laid a hand gently on Wendell's shoulder to reassure him.

# 13

# The Grave News

## WAXING GIBBOUS MOON

The next morning, Jacques woke up sore and stared at the ceiling for a few moments. He eased himself upright, slowly shifting his legs to the side of the bed and standing with a groan as his body protested the movement. Katharina had suggested stretching to gently work his muscles and restore his arm. He took out some fresh clothes and filled the empty tub with water from the spigot outside, then lit the bed of coals underneath the tub to warm it up. As the water heated, he stripped down and stepped in, letting his body adjust to the temperature. Leaning his head back, he let out a long, slow breath and closed his eyes.

Nightmare's face, bony and matted, appeared behind his eyelids. Jacques opened his eyes and gasped. His hands gripped the sides of the basin. When the vision faded, he focused on his breathing like Katharina had told him. Once settled, he inspected his upper arm. The holes were now pinched together, leaving small, jagged scars with a dip in between where a chunk had gone missing thanks to the point of the monster's antlers. He could hardly lift it above his head or carry heavy objects, though he had been exercising daily as the midwife suggested. Multicolored bruises still dotted his skin; more reminders of what he had endured that night.

His gaze lowered to his abdomen, aching and still thin where the creature had bit into him. He remembered Obstein telling him that the skin would grow back with time. Jacques mused that he should visit the apothecary to ensure his wounds were healing properly.

Then he studied an older wound on his chest. Obstein hadn't mentioned it, but Jacques was sure the doctor had observed it while patching him up. Though mostly healed, it still left a divot and small scar that time could not erase. As he stared at it, the distant sound of gunshots resounded within his mind. He once again gripped the sides of the tub, knuckles straining against the skin. His body tensed, painful and sharp. The muscles in his legs fluttered and squeezed, ready for use.

"Jacques?"

He startled, splashing water over the floor. Recognizing Wendell's voice through the door, he let out a breath.

"Are you well?" Wendell asked.

"I'm almost done," Jacques responded in a breathless rush. Whether he was well or not was a question he could not answer. He scrubbed his body quickly with soap, dunking his head underwater and running his hands through it to get out any dirt or grime stuck within his tresses. After rinsing the soap off, he climbed out of the tub and wrapped himself with a towel. He opened the door after gathering his clothes. "Sorry for making you wait."

Wendell's gaze was focused on his face—as if seeing him for the first time. Those large eyes were wide, as if they were staring straight into Jacques' soul. Water dripped down his back from the damp strands, some of which clung to his cheek and neck. He didn't know how Wendell saw him, with a towel loosely wrapped around his hips and his garish wounds exposed, but he noticed a pink tinge to Wendell's pale cheeks and ears and the way his throat bobbed when he swallowed.

Jacques averted his gaze and walked past him, into the room he had been staying in once he was well enough to move around more. He dried off, pulling on a fresh tunic and pants that once belonged to Hansel. He felt vulnerable with his scars and bruises showing, repulsive in his own skin.

He sat with his head in his hands, trying to disperse the images in his mind and mute the sounds he never wanted to hear again. The pounding grew louder, but it was not inside his head. Someone was knocking at the front door. Jacques stood warily and walked slowly and silently down the hallway, avoiding the floorboards that creaked the most. As he passed by the kitchen, he palmed a knife. Peering through the thin slats of the shutters, he saw doctor Obstein standing on the porch. Other villagers plodded down the path toward the center of town. Snow was shoveled to the side and melting. None of them were staring at Wendell's house or loitering about in the streets, as Jacques almost expected. He didn't spot the group of newcomers, so he deemed it safe to greet the doctor. He hid the knife behind his back and opened the door just a crack.

"Doctor, are you here to check on my wounds?" he asked casually.

Obstein appeared to have something else in mind, but said, "Yes, and I would like to discuss something with Wendell."

"Is it about the Inquisitors?" Jacques asked, his hand tightening on the knife. His eyes scanned the area for the newcomers.

"You are very astute, Jacques," Obstein replied. "It is just me. I thought it would be best to talk with Wendell alone before introducing them."

"I won't let them near him until I know they mean no harm," Jacques declared fervently. He gripped the edge of the door, prepared to slam it shut at any moment.

Obstein's eyes softened, and he gave Jacques a warm smile. "I admire your protectiveness of Wendell," he said. "Albrecht would be happy to know you kept your oath to him."

Jacques felt his hold on the knife loosen as he focused on the doctor. He opened the door fully, stepping aside. "Come in."

"Thank you," Obstein said with a nod of his head. "First, let us see your injuries." He walked into the main area and placed his medical bag on the long wooden table, pulling out tools.

Jacques sat in a chair close to the table and began lifting his tunic above his head. His left arm ached, trembling as he extricated it from the opening in the fabric. Obstein observed him, his eyes drifting to his right hand. Jacques was still holding the knife and set it down gently on the table.

"I see you are prepared for whatever may come for him," Obstein murmured. "Or is it simply an old habit?"

Jacques had no response, pursing his lips tightly. He was silent as the doctor prodded at his healing arm, peering at the scabbed-over skin. "Almost fully healed," he said to himself. Jacques straightened as the doctor examined his stomach. "And this is recovering nicely." The doctor looked at his patient. "How are you feeling?"

For the second time that day, Jacques had difficulty answering such a question. Thankfully, he didn't have to; Wendell padded into the room and noticed them.

"Doctor Obstein!" he greeted the doctor brightly.

"Ah, Wendell. Please join us," the doctor said.

Jacques watched Wendell take a seat next to him, knowing his face was pale and open as a book. Wendell peered at him, his smile fading, and then turned back to Obstein.

"What's going on?" Wendell asked.

"There has been word regarding your grandfather," Obstein said grimly. He waited for Wendell to absorb his words before continuing in a soft tone, "I'm sorry, my child, but he passed during his travels."

Wendell's face turned ashen, his mouth opening slightly and tears forming in his eyes. Jacques placed a hand gently on Wendell's back, rubbing slow circles against the rough fabric of the tunic. "I'm so sorry, Wendy," he whispered.

Wendell sucked in a large breath, the only movement after sitting unnaturally still after Obstein spoke. He was staring ahead, but his gaze was far off. Stiffly, he stood and began trudging away. Jacques rose to go after him, but Obstein shook his head curtly.

Wendell walked down the hall, pausing at the doorway to his grandfather's room. He always held onto the hope that he would see the old man again, but there was also an aching feeling deep in his chest that he wouldn't. Hearing the doctor confirm what he dreaded was still hard, and he needed a moment to mourn by himself.

Wendell pushed open the door and walked inside, taking in the belongings left behind. Each item contained a precious memory of the man who cared for him when no one else did.

He remembered sitting in his grandfather's lap as a young boy, one hand stroking his hair gently while the other held a booklet that he read from. It was a fable about a proud hare and a humble tortoise. Wendell was always enamored by the resilience of the slower tortoise.

"Do you think they will let me play with them today, Grandfather?" he would ask each day. The other children usually shunned him or became violent when he tried to join in on their games, yet he yearned to laugh and run like they did in the streets.

His grandfather would smile and lean down to pat his head. "Maybe. You just have to try," he would respond. No matter what, he always gave Wendell the confidence that one day he would be accepted by the village and the rest of his family.

His vision blurred as he approached the worktable. The clock they started building together was left unfinished. Wendell touched the wood gently, examining it silently, turning it over in his hands to feel the texture of the carvings. Tears dropped onto the table, mixing with dust. Soon his forehead met the wooden surface as he sobbed, holding the clock tightly.

# 14

# The Right Questions

The next few days were blissfully peaceful, and Jacques almost dared to believe they would be left alone from then on. He cursed when he saw the Inquisitors coming down the road toward the house one morning, with Father Heinrich leading the way. He ran to Wendell's room with his heart pounding as loud as his feet on the floorboards. "Wendell, they're coming. We must get you out of here!" he called, flinging open the door.

Wendell was sitting on his bed, reading a book he had borrowed from the library. He had been reclusive since Obstein told him of his grandfather's passing, keeping to himself in his room to mourn or reading to keep his mind from dwelling on the loss. He watched Jacques' frenzied approach with a resigned demeanor. "I can't leave, remember?" he replied. "The curse will follow me, and then no one will be safe."

"Well, you can't just let them kill you!" Jacques spluttered, spreading out his arms in agitation. He didn't know why Wendell was acting so blasé about a group of witch hunters at his doorstep. "We have to do something, try to reason with them, whatever it takes!" He paced around the room, waving his arms around wildly. Wendell simply stared at him with wide eyes, blinking owlishly at him. "Listen," he said in a softer tone and stopped pacing, walking closer to the bed. "I want to help you. You saved my life—"

"I almost killed you," Wendell interrupted him, eyebrows raised.

Jacques sighed, placing a comforting hand on Wendell's shoulder. "You didn't, though."

"I have killed others, and I will kill again if we cannot find a way to dispel this curse," Wendell said. Jacques could see the guilt in his expression and hear regret in his voice.

A loud knocking on the front door made Jacques jerk. He stood with a determined expression. "I'm not going to let them hurt you. I'll fight them all off if I must."

"But what if they can *help*," Wendell said, setting his book aside and rising. His voice was pleading, desperate.

"I doubt that's what they're here for," Jacques grumbled. There was another knock, louder this time. "Stay here for now, until I know it's safe," he told Wendell.

The other seemed as if he wanted to object, but Jacques gently cupped his face and brushed his thumb along Wendell's cheek in re-assurance as he held his cervine eyes with his own. "Please, just trust me," he said in a softer tone.

Wendell nodded and sat back down on his bed.

Setting his mouth in a grim line, Jacques marched out of the room and toward the door. He searched through the house for any weapons he could use against the group as the knocking persisted, getting louder. Jacques thought they would break the door down. He noticed Hansel's hunting rifle near the door and reached for it.

When he opened the door, he had a firm glare fixed upon his face. The warm, excited smile that greeted him changed that into a dumbfounded expression.

"Hello! I'm Anna. Are you Wendell?" Her accent was pronounced, and it was clear she did not speak much of his language.

Determined not to let her false cheer take his guard down, he growled, "No, now leave," and slammed the door, putting his back against it and clutching the rifle to his chest.

"That's Jacques, a traveler who came into town recently," he heard Father Heinrich explain on the other side of the door, voice muffled. "He was injured by the creature."

"Then why is he here?" Jacques heard the Inquisitor called Luis ask, his voice low and dark.

Father Heinrich answered again. "Wendell and his grandfather tended to his wounds. He stayed with them while his wounds healed. I suspect he feels as if he owes them a debt."

"Will you let us in?" Irving said in a calm tone.

"No! Leave us alone!" Jacques yelled back.

"We do not intend to harm anyone," Irving replied. Jacques was quiet as he listened. "We just want to figure out more about the curse. Please let us speak with Wendell."

"I don't trust you!" Jacques snarled, tightening his grip around the rifle.

"You don't have to trust us," a voice spoke up from beside him and he jumped, seeing a short man standing nearby.

"How did you get in?" Jacques exclaimed, hastily pointing the gun at the man's chest.

"The window was unlocked," Luis said with a shrug. He had his arms crossed against his chest and a glare in his eyes. "Now put the weapon down and open the door."

Jacques watched him warily, cornered between him and the door. He wondered which was the bigger threat, keeping the gun trained on Luis for now. He expected the others to come charging through the door at any moment. "If you're here to kill him, I'm not going to let that happen." He emphasized his resolve by moving his finger toward the trigger, peering down the barrel to line up a fatal shot.

"That would be our last resort," Irving said, sticking his head through the open window. Luis was staring at Jacques instead of the rifle aimed for his heart. "We are here to determine if there is a way to kill the creature itself without harming Wendell. There are no guarantees, however."

Jacques shook his head, still staring down Luis. "I can't put my faith in that. I don't believe you won't hurt him." Despite the sweat building up in his palms, his hold on the rifle remained steady.

"I'm sorry you feel that way, but we have traveled a long way for this purpose, and we shall not be dissuaded so easily," Irving said resolutely and gave a subtle nod that caused Jacques to divert his attention. Before he could reply, he felt himself falling.

The wind rushed out of his lungs as he hit the floor hard. The gun was ripped from his hands, yanking his shoulder back. Jacques wrapped an arm around his stomach, over the wound that was still healing, and hissed in pain.

Luis stood over him, holding the gun. "Do we have to restrain you, or are you going to cooperate?"

Jacques struggled to get up, but his arm still wasn't fully healed to support all his weight while the other clutched his middle. Instead, he simply glared up at the man, teeth clenched, almost bared. "Go to hell," he spat.

"I'll take that as a no," the Inquisitor stepped over him and opened the door, letting the rest of his group in. Father Heinrich made the sign of the cross as he entered, stepping around Jacques with a frightened expression. A few townsfolk stood outside, peering in curiously as they strained to see what was happening.

"You bastards! All of you!" Jacques called out to them from his position on the floor. "You're so willing to give up another person's life just to live more comfortably?" The villagers tittered and muttered to themselves, beginning to turn away. "If anything happens to him, it's all your fault!" he yelled at their retreating backs. "If anything happens, I'll avenge him myself!"

"God help us," Father Heinrich murmured, clutching his rosary.

"Calm down," Luis said, nudging Jacques with his foot. "We already told you we're not here to kill him. If you just listen, things will go much smoother for all of us."

"We didn't ask you to come here," Jacques hissed, sitting up. His arms shook with the effort.

"No, but someone else did," Irving noted, glancing down at him.

Jacques cut his eyes to the clergyman, who was staring at him as if a demon had crawled up from hell.

"We talked to Albrecht." Irving stated with a knowing aspect.

Wendell heard the commotion in the foyer and felt his chest tighten, breath hitching as panic began to rise within him. He cautiously got up from the bed where he had been waiting and walked slowly toward his door. Concern for his friend warred with his fear of the unknown enemy within his home. He reached out for the doorknob, hoping to open it just a smidge to get a peek down the hall.

Instead, it opened before he could turn the knob. A woman dressed in riding breeches and a blouse let out a noise of surprise when she saw him, then smiled brightly. "Ah, you must be Wendell."

He lurched back with a gasp, startled by her sudden appearance. She reached out to him with concern in her eyes. "My apologies for scaring you, we just want to talk."

Wendell fought his instinct to flee, instead fisting his hands and clenching his jaw. "What did you do to Jacques?" He hoped his tone was stronger than he felt in that moment.

"Hm?" She quirked her head to the side, then glanced behind her. A large man appeared, gruff and hairy. Wendell swallowed a lump in his throat as he stared up at him.

The man simply jerked his chin in the direction of the entryway.

"Oh, is that your friend? He seems very protective of you," Anna said and winked at him.

Unsure what to do and beginning to hyperventilate, Wendell glanced past the two Inquisitors down the hall to see if he could catch a glimpse of Jacques.

She held out her hand to him, which he studied warily as if she had claws. It was like she wanted him to come with them.

Wendell briefly considered his options. He had little choice but to follow them to the front room. He saw muddied boot prints on the floor near the door and frowned at the dirt. Searching around, he finally spotted Jacques—he was being restrained by one of the Inquisitors, his hands behind his back and fabric in his mouth, muffling his words.

"Jacques!" Wendell rushed toward him.

"He was giving us trouble, so we had to tie him up," the Inquisitor stated.

"Let him go!" Wendell cried out, grabbing for the bonds. "He's still injured, you're hurting him." He tugged the gag out of Jacques' mouth who coughed, licking his lips. The other man let go, stepping away as Wendell hastily undid the ropes around Jacques' wrists.

"I'm sorry, Wendy, I tried to stop them," Jacques gasped out, rubbing his shoulder. Seeing Jacques wince in pain ignited a fire within Wendell he was unaware had lain dormant inside of him. He had tended to the man's wounds himself, nursing him back to health for so long that seeing it come undone by another's hands set off alarm bells in his head.

"Well, you must be Wendell," one of the Inquisitors spoke to him, this one taller and resembling the larger man who had been at his bedroom door.

Wendell felt fury for the first time in his life, an unbridled rage that threatened to tear him apart, as he whirled around to face the man. "Get out," he growled. He didn't recognize his own voice. It was rough and sharp.

"We only want to speak with you," the man replied calmly.

His demeanor only made Wendell angrier. "You come into my home unannounced and threaten us by force," Wendell hissed. He glared at the man, fists shaking at his sides. The room darkened as if clouds were passing overhead, and the air grew tense. It felt like a storm was brewing in the house itself. The Inquisitors glanced around with alert eyes and stiffened bodies, expecting an attack. "Leave," Wendell commanded. "And do not dare return."

Wendell had never threatened anyone before. His entire life he had made himself as small and unassuming as possible to avoid the cruel accusations his neighbors threw at him for being a murderer. He always used a soft voice and polite mannerisms so people wouldn't be frightened by his mere existence. Now, however, he used the fear and apprehension that had always surrounded him to his advantage.

He saw the expressions on the Inquisitors change from calm and confident to wary unease. They weren't quite the faces of terror he was hoping for, but his warning was enough to make them back off. The tall man held up his hands in surrender and the others shuffled out of the house with quiet apologies.

Jacques scowled out of the window. The Inquisitors were scouring the village, attempting to speak with anyone they saw. They proceeded back and forth between the church and the apothecary for a few days, according to Katharina. She still came by to check on his wounds and report on their movements, per his request. Apparently, they had a lot of questions about the nature of the curse and the beast it produced—both theological and medical.

"What are they doing now?" Wendell asked gently. He was meek after the intrusion, treading softly across the floor.

"They appear to be harassing the rest of the village, now," Jacques muttered. He was surprised at Wendell's reaction to the Inquisitors, at the fury in his eyes and bite to his words when he told them to leave. He expected the mild-mannered young man to be fearful or to flee at the confrontation, but instead, he showed tenacity. It warmed Jacques' heart to see the fierce resistance Wendell displayed—perhaps he did not need to be coddled and protected from the dangers of the world. Still, Jacques would not leave him to fend for himself. They agreed that Wendell would stay inside the house, away from the witch hunters and curious villagers.

"I'm going out," Jacques added. "I want to know their true intentions."

Wendell pursed his lips, eyebrows knitting together. "Be careful out there," he whispered. Jacques nodded at him and then exited the house.

"Aye, they asked me about Wendell," Stuber grumbled. His eyes squinted in distrust, belying his foul mood. "And of those who were cursed before him."

Jacques had approached the innkeeper to inquire about the group. "What did they say?" he asked.

Stuber waved a disgruntled hand. "Asked too many questions, more like. It's not right for strangers to know this much. I don't like it."

The sentiment was shared by the rest of the village. They preferred to live out their lives with the curse quietly haunting them, occasionally allowing a wandering traveler to succumb to death in their stead or welcoming a new family to spare an older one from harboring the burden. Distrustful, easily ruffled, and malignant were the people who lived here. Jacques was starting to understand why the longer he stayed.

## FULL MOON

A few nights later, a howl pierced the night air and Wendell's back stiffened, a chill rushing through him and raising the small hairs on his arms. It was a sound the village rarely heard, due to the decay surrounding them that made most animals avoid the area. Whatever predators tried to claim the territory were usually picked off by Nightmare or had too much trouble finding fresh food due to the unhealthy soil. The starved shells of wolves and bears often turned up on the outskirts of the forest, their emaciated forms leaving little meat for the villagers to harvest.

Jacques' head whipped up at the sound and he flung himself at the window, peering out into the night. "What is that?" he asked.

Wendell swallowed, forcing his body to calm. "Must be a wolf," he said. "They're uncommon around here, but not unheard of."

Jacques' forehead was creased, his eyebrows coming together as he shook his head. "That doesn't sound like any wolf I've heard," he murmured.

His words sent a jolt of fear coursing through Wendell once again. It was unusual for a wolf to prowl their forest, of course, but the way Jacques said it made it seem like something was wrong. "What do you think it could be?" he asked around a knot in his throat. The shelves within the town hall's library had some information on local flora and fauna, which was about as much as Wendell had to go off. Some of the animals mentioned within the books he had only seen through illustrations, let alone heard their calls.

Jacques had his jaw clenched, still peering outside as if he could see what was making the noise. Wendell approached the window slowly, standing beside him and staring through the glass past his reflection made by the candlelight. His eyesight could pick up more details than Jacques' probably could, and the illumination of the moon helped to outline objects and the tree lines. Still, he couldn't see the creature. He wondered if this was how the villagers felt when Nightmare was out stalking the woods.

"A fox, maybe?" he offered. He glanced at Jacques, who didn't seem convinced, but leaned away from the window.

"Maybe," he conceded, his eyebrows still knitted together and lips pursed. He placed his hands on his hips. "Let's not worry about it. Food's getting cold." He gestured for Wendell to join him as he made his way back to the table, where their food waited.

# 15

# The True Motives

## WANING GIBBOUS MOON

**The Inquisitors petitioned to meet** with Jacques and Wendell once again and set things right. Obstein agreed to mediate between the two parties as an unbiased voice. They met at the town hall, empty save for a few silent caretakers. The four travelers were already at the Hall when Jacques and Wendell entered with Obstein. A table and several chairs were set up in the center of the room to accommodate everyone. Jacques spotted Anna scanning a nearby bookshelf with interest, while Irving and Luis were sitting next to each other, facing the entrance. The other man was leaning against the wall, arms crossed over his chest. Irving stood when they approached, but Luis remained lounging.

"I'm afraid we did this all wrong," Irving announced. "We shouldn't have forced our way into your home, and for that, I apologize." Jacques thought he sounded like the diplomats trying to preach unification of the land. "Let's start over with proper introductions.

My name is Irving," the tall blond man continued, reaching out a hand to Wendell and Jacques. When neither of them moved to shake it, he continued. "This is Anna," he gestured to the smiling woman who hurried to stand beside him. She wiggled her fingers in greeting. "My brother, Michael," he gestured to the larger man leaning against the wall, who nodded his head slightly. "And Luis. He's crude but effective." Irving's fingers rested lightly on the shorter man's shoulders, glancing at him with a small smile. Luis scowled up at him but did not shake Irving's hand off his shoulder.

"Doctor Obstein told me you met my grandfather," Wendell said to Irving. He was stiff but willing to hear them out after having some time to cool down after their last interaction.

Irving's face grew full of sorrow. "Yes, we happened to be in the same town as him and heard that he was searching for a way to end a curse. I must express my deepest condolences," he said and bowed his head, closing his eyes and placing a hand over his chest in a genuine gesture.

"Your grandfather was very ill by the time we spoke with him and seemed to be aging rapidly," Anna explained in English, with Irving translating. "I did everything I could to help him, but I think it may have been too late at that point. He told us everything he knew about the situation and spoke about you often."

Wendell understood a bit of what she said, having read some English texts and listened to merchants speak the language as they came through. "Thank you," Wendell told her in stilting English. "For being there in his last moments."

The group gave solemnity toward Wendell with their expressions. Anna stepped forward to embrace him, and he was taken by surprise. The only person who had ever hugged him like that before was now gone. Slowly, he hugged her back, arms wrapping around her awkwardly and face pressed against her collarbone. The oddity of the embrace turned to comfort and warmth. He cried as she smoothed his hair with her hand, pressing her cheek to his head.

"I must admit to our deceit," Irving stated. After the emotional moment, the group had settled down amongst the couches and chairs within the Hall. At Irving's words, Jacques and Wendell stared at him quizzically.

"What deceit?" Jacques asked with an edge to his voice. He was still wary of the group and stayed close by Wendell's side.

"We are not truly Inquisitors," Irving whispered, leaning in secretively. "Well, Michael and I are not anymore," he clarified, sitting back against the cushions. "We pretended to be sent by the church so the townspeople would assist us." Beside him, Luis gave a snort of annoyance to imply that the villagers were not helpful at all.

"What are you, then?" Wendell asked curiously, while Jacques tensed beside him.

Irving glanced at Michael and Anna, hesitating. "We are hunters, in a sense," Irving told them.

"But we do not hunt witches," Anna added, holding a finger up. "We seek to stop curses or ailments that are caused by supernatural means."

"Since the church is aggressively seeking out any hint of witchcraft, we act as Inquisitors to blend in," Luis explained. Michael dipped his head in agreement.

Wendell turned to Jacques with wide eyes. "Then it *is* true," he said in awe. "Others like me are out there; your bards were right."

Jacques blinked in surprise, then turned back to the group. "What manner of beast or plague have you encountered?"

Irving settled a bit further into his seat next to Luis, casually draping an arm across the back of the couch behind the other man. "We call them shapeshifters—people who turn into creatures—they are usually cursed or were made that way by unnatural forces. We try to help them when we can."

"Fascinating," Obstein murmured to himself. He was writing in a notebook, the pen scratching swiftly across the blank pages as they talked.

"How do you find them?" Wendell asked, leaning forward. His eyes were bright and hopeful, the pupils dilating.

Irving answered him. "We listen for news of strange beasts and unusual attacks or simply follow the trail of Inquisitors on the hunt for witches. Sometimes there is nothing to the rumors, other times we encounter them directly."

"And sometimes we help people wrongfully accused of witchcraft escape a hanging or burning at the stake," Luis added, glancing at Anna with a half smile.

"I was almost burned at the stake, once," she admitted conspiratorially. She had a wistful expression on her face. "The city thought I was a witch trying to poison their youth and seduce their husbands. All I did was make poultices and potions for their minor aches and ailments. Of course, I messed up a few times when I was still learning, and there were some dreadful consequences, though I was getting better at it!" she explained fervently. "But they had a fever no poultice could remedy and were burning people accused of witchcraft with barely a thought. Neighbors, friends, family members; once someone was accused, they became something other than what they had been their whole lives." She shook her head. "I was in a cart being taken to the square when these two came running in, demanding they stop the burnings." She gestured to Irving and Michael. "The city didn't like that, however," she laughed. "They ended up being run out of town, but during the commotion I was able to escape. We met up on the outskirts."

"So, you're really a witch?" Jacques asked.

Anna cackled. "Some call it witchcraft, but I consider it medicine much like what your apothecary or midwife does." She gestured to Doctor Obstein.

"Anna has helped us create treatments for shapeshifters and those afflicted with curses," Irving stated. "We were hoping that, with your cooperation, she could find a way to separate Nightmare from you." He gazed at Wendell with sincerity in his eyes. "From there, we can combat the beast without any harm coming to you."

Wendell shook his head. "It will simply move to another person. The people of this village have tried expelling the beast in several ways, but it was of no use."

"I am afraid he is right," Obstein added. He set his notes down on a side table and folded his hands over his lap. "To my knowledge, Nightmare cannot be separated from its human counterpart, which may mean it cannot subsist on its own, but it has found ways to latch onto the people here and be reborn."

Luis turned to Jacques. "You came face to face with it and lived. What can you tell us about it?"

Jacques' palms clammed up as the memories resurfaced. "It's difficult to remember," he admitted. "It was huge, with many antlers. Like a giant stag, but wrong."

"How so?" Anna asked, quirking her head toward him.

"It looked like it was already dead. I saw its ribs sticking out," Jacques shook his head, pressing a hand to his forehead and squeezing his eyes shut.

"We have some descriptions of the creature from other close encounters," Obstein stated, peering over at Jacques briefly. "It is as Jacques says: the beast does not appear normal or to be living." He pursed his lips. "However, one thing we have known from the beginning is that it leaves a trail of death wherever it goes; not just the sacrifice."

"Are you referring to the withered trees and plants in the forest, or the rotten soil all around the village?" Luis suggested.

Obstein tilted his head in acknowledgement. "Yes, it kills whatever it touches. Our crops have died, and we have had to move our fields and livestock several times to avoid Nightmare's trail."

"Father Heinrich says it demands a sacrifice each month," Wendell added softly. "If one is not made, plagues befall the village, and many people die."

They all watched Jacques. He squirmed under their intense gazes. Wendell placed a reassuring hand on his shoulder, hoping to settle his nerves.

"And yet you survived," Luis said. He was idly rubbing a finger along his moustache, though his eyes were scrutinizing.

"With wounds and all," Anna added with raised brows.

Jacques was rigid, his muscles tensed as the outline of thick veins bulged on his skin. His eyes were fearful, as if reliving the experience.

"He is the only one," Obstein told them, keeping a careful eye on Jacques. The group turned to the doctor, and Jacques let out a breath. "Those who go near the creature usually grow ill or age faster than the rest of us. When Albrecht brought Jacques to me, I could see the difference plain as day." He eyed Wendell and said softly, "The touch of death was upon him even before he left the village."

Anna's face scrunched up and she mumbled something to herself, too low to make out. Her hands moved to her face, fingers tapping against her chin in thought. "Everything you've said leads to death and decay," she said louder. "That is the curse in action, yes?"

Wendell gazed up at Anna and nodded his head. "Yes, that is what we believe." She met his stare, a grin spreading across her face.

Luis rolled his neck, sighing. "I know that look," he said, glancing at Irving as he leaned further back into his seat.

Irving's forehead was creased, his lips downturned. "A curse of instant death? But how can that be?" he asked.

"This is no ordinary being, Irving!" Anna exclaimed, strangely cheerful given the situation. Her eyes were alight with excitement.

"Oh, this is a fun one, I cannot wait to get started!"

Irving held up a hand to her, still with that hard face. "We have to be careful; this is beyond the realm of what we are used to dealing with." Michael hummed in affirmation.

"We've faced monsters before, what's so different about this one?" Luis asked from his lounging spot.

Irving cut his eyes to him. "This is not the same as a werewolf, Luis," he said, exasperated.

The two stared heatedly at each other as they argued the hazards of monsters and unknown misfortunes. Jacques watched them with trepidation and concern. Anna ignored them and shuffled closer to Wendell, who shifted a bit closer to Jacques.

"Can you communicate with it?" she asked in a rush, her expression brimming with glee. She had to repeat a few words for Wendell to understand.

"With Nightmare? No, I—I've never tried," Wendell stammered.

"And you cannot control the transformations?" she said inquisitively, peering at him closely.

Wendell shook his head. "It just . . . happens. Every night there is a new moon."

"Well then, we'll just have to wait for the next one, I suppose," she said with a smile and plopped back into her seat.

"Absolutely not!" Wendell exclaimed with finality, reeling away from her. The Hall went silent as everyone's attention shifted to the two of them.

Anna cocked her head to the side, mouth in a small pout. "Why not?"

"It's too dangerous!" Wendell was shaking his head vigorously. "You'll die the instant you go near it!"

"Jacques didn't," Luis spoke up, sitting forward with his elbows on his knees. He studied Jacques for a moment, then shifted his gaze back to Wendell. "Besides, we'd just be observing from afar."

Anna turned to the doctor. "You said Albrecht spoke with it on the night Jacques was wounded."

"I believe he tried, but I am unsure whether it can speak or communicate in any manner," he replied.

"Perhaps we can get it to speak through Wendell—" she began.

"No, I can't," Wendell stood abruptly, his whole body shaking. "I'm sorry, but you're asking too much of me right now." His hands clenched into fists at his sides, nails digging into his palms. His breathing had accelerated, and perspiration began to gather on his skin.

Jacques reached out to him, but Wendell left in a rush. He rose to go after him, but the doctor waved his hand. "Not to worry, he will settle down. He has had an excitable condition since he was very young." He reprimanded Anna sternly, "Please be careful not to incite a panic in him again."

Anna sheepishly ducked her head, then gasped and quickly turned to Jacques. "Then if you're willing, maybe we can see if you can talk to it!"

Jacques startled, shifting back, his eyes widening. "I'd rather not," he said plainly.

Luis sighed and nudged Anna, shaking his head at her. She gave him a quizzical expression, as if unaware of her wrongdoing. Michael had an amused smile.

"Let us take our leave for now," Irving suggested, glancing at the alarm and wariness on Jacques' face. He gestured to the doctor. "Thank you for introducing us." His eyes fell upon Jacques. "And thank you for agreeing to aid us. Please give Wendell our apologies for alarming him. We will give him space before continuing our discussions."

Jacques stood and shook Irving's offered hand this time. Luis got up and followed Irving out with Michael and Anna. She waved before exiting the Hall.

The place felt much larger with just Jacques and the doctor left, yet the air was still heavy around them. Jacques had anticipated a conversation with the doctor once they were alone. Obstein was still seated, so Jacques eased himself back down, preparing for what the man would say next.

"While you are here, there is a small matter I wish to address regarding your health, Sir Lorrain." Doctor Obstein observed Jacques with a peculiar expression—knowledge in his eyes.

Jacques swallowed, clenching his jaw and tightening his limbs. The urge to run overtook him again, but this time he didn't know if he would ever stop. Despite that, he stayed still and silent, waiting for the doctor to reveal what knowledge he held.

"I was not concerned with it at the time of your first bloody arrival to my apothecary, but during later examinations, Katharina and I discovered another wound. An older one." The doctor took out a round, silver ball. "Upon your back there is a scar that I have seen many times before in fallen soldiers on the field, caused by a bullet such as this," Obstein continued, holding the object up between his thumb and forefinger. "And upon your chest there is a matching wound. When I have examined these soldiers, I have seen the damage wrought upon their insides. Some have survived with near misses, but quickly succumb to infection and die."

Jacques knew what the doctor was referring to. He remembered the day clearly—gunpowder and smoke in the air, the smell of upturned earth and a ringing in his ears. He had felt a sharp, fast blow to his back and stumbled forward with the impact. His hands had hit the soiled grass, and in front of him was blood and other gory bits soaking into the ground. A shaking hand had felt his chest and come back red.

"I believe you should have died before ever setting foot in this village, young man." Obstein was staring at him, expecting an explanation that Jacques could not give. "And if not then, you should have died as soon as you encountered Nightmare. Yet here you are."

"Yes," Jacques said, unsteady. He swallowed thickly and averted his gaze down to his hands, wringing them. "Here I am. I do not know why or how. You are right, Doctor, I should have died then. Our medic said the bullet should have gone straight through my heart and killed me immediately." He breathed in, then out. "That is why I had to run. The way he looked at me; I knew it wasn't right, what happened. But I couldn't stay. They would have thought me a monster."

"You must tell the hunters about this," Obstein said with an expectant expression. He had a fatherly air about him, which eased Jacques' nerves a bit.

Jacques scrunched up his face, continuing to fidget. "But what if they think I'm damned as well?"

"If what we believe is true, then perhaps there is a chance to overcome this plight. You could be the key to unlocking a mystery that has surrounded this area for hundreds of years."

Jacques stared at the calluses on his fingers, still seeing the blood from the wound on his hands. "What do you think I am?" he asked, voice faltering. He finally returned his gaze to the physician, unsure of his reaction and whether he wanted to know how the man felt about him.

Doctor Obstein met his eyes. "I think you are a man who cannot die."

# 16

# The Pleasant Meal

**The group came to Wendell's** home the next afternoon. As Irving stated the night before, they did not rush headlong into discussing the curse.

"I must ask your forgiveness again for our behavior yesterday," Irving began with a small bow to Wendell and Jacques. He gave a piercing stare at Anna, who ducked her head guiltily. "So, I thought we could have a good meal and get to know one another better."

Jacques and Wendell exchanged a glance. They had been running low on food supplies, with local merchants wary to sell their wares to either of them. Bäcker still hadn't forgiven Jacques for stealing bread the day he left town, and Fleischer was difficult to haggle with.

"Oh," Wendell said. "That sounds nice." He was calmer today, less wary of the strangers.

"I'll get the tea on," Luis said as he went into the kitchen.

Michael carried in a large hunk of pork procured from the butcher and started to prepare it. As Anna walked by with her bag in hand, she took out a small container filled with herbs and flower petals.

"I made this last night when Doctor Obstein explained your condition. Whenever you feel anxious, just open this jar and take a deep breath," she said as she handed it to Wendell, mimicking what she was describing to him. "It always helps me calm down when I'm worked up."

"Thank you, I'm sorry for—" Wendell said but was cut off.

"No need! I'm the one who should be apologizing," Anna told him with a wave of her hand. "Sometimes I get carried away when doing research." She ran a hand through her hair, which was freshly washed and brushed.

Wendell smiled at her, appreciating her easygoing nature. She patted his back and entered the kitchen, setting her bag down and producing ingredients for the meal. Soon the house was filled with wondrous smells and a familiar warmth. Irving and Jacques set plates on the table, which Luis occupied as soon as he finished brewing the tea. He gestured for Wendell to sit down with him, passing him a cup and pouring tea into it. Jacques disappeared back into the kitchen.

"Irving called me 'crude and effective' yesterday, but I'd rather you form your own opinion," Luis said and took a sip. "So, I thought I'd share my story with you."

Wendell's eyes lit up. "I would love to hear it, but you don't have to tell me if you'd rather not."

Luis shrugged and took another sip of tea, the steam wafting up into the air. "I was born in Spain to a family that was too large and too poor to put food on the table. Many of my siblings died of illness and starvation, while my elders were persecuted for their faith. I took to the streets, stealing food and money wherever I could."

Wendell listened carefully, wrapping his hands around his warm mug. "I'm sorry you lost your family that young; it must have been awful."

Luis sighed, his head slightly bent. "You weren't the one dragging my grandparents out of our home and throwing them in jail for heresy. That was the *real* Inquisition."

"Ah, telling him about your childhood?" Irving said as he sat down next to Luis with a smile. He poured a cup of tea for himself.

"You said we should get to know each other," Luis replied, spreading his arms out.

Irving took a sip, hiding his grin behind the cup. "Yes, do continue."

Luis turned back to Wendell. "As I was saying, I didn't want to be a burden anymore, and my parents urged me to leave. I only had a few siblings left, and they were doing their best to take care of everyone. So, I ran."

"Not very far, though," Irving remarked. He leaned back in his chair, relaxing.

"No, not really. I still wanted to keep an eye on them, so I ended up at sea." Luis admitted. "I signed on to a merchant vessel and sneaked them food and clothing whenever I could after a voyage. I was almost caught a few times."

Wendell grinned. "That sounds like a fellow from England I've read tales about, they called him Robin Hood."

Irving threw his head back and laughed, while Luis furrowed his eyebrows. "Tell him about your reputation." Irving nudged him with a wry smile.

Luis rolled his eyes and groused, "I will if you stop interrupting."

Wendell grinned at the playfulness of Irving's tone and did not miss the small smile on Luis's lips. It was a completely different aura than when they first met; the facade had lifted, revealing their true selves.

"I suppose I became a known criminal," Luis shrugged nonchalantly. By the expression on Irving's face, Wendell could tell this was an understatement. "Others heard of me helping my family and started asking for help, too. At first, I didn't want to risk it. Missing wares would be noticed after time went by." Luis's lips twitched up a bit into a proud smirk. "But then we were accosted by British privateers. The merchant I was apprenticing under was killed, and we were asked whether we wanted to join *him* or *them*." He lifted his hands and grinned fully. "For me, it was an easy choice. So, I became a privateer."

Wendell's eyes widened; his mouth slightly open. "Like Sir Francis Drake? I read about him, too."

Irving and Luis exchanged looks that Wendell could not decipher. "You could say so," Luis said, stroking his thin goatee. "When I told the captain what I did, he agreed to send some of the prizes we won to my home. Then we started smuggling families out of Spain. We had a network throughout the Mediterranean and Caribbean."

"Sounds like quite the adventure," Wendell said in an awed voice. It felt like he was meeting one of the heroes from the stories he read so avidly, which seemed so grandiose and full of embellishments. But here Luis was in real life, an adventurer right before Wendell's eyes.

Luis shook his head, losing the playful tone. "Not quite. Our network did not last long. It was discovered by the Spanish Crown. At that point, I had become too well known to stay and needed to flee again or face the hangman's noose. I sailed to England, where I met Irving and Michael as they were investigating the witch hunts in the area." Luis glanced at Irving with a fond smile.

"At first he wanted nothing to do with us, but eventually I—er, *we*—won him over," Irving said, cheeks slightly flushed. His hand had drifted to rest lightly on Luis's shoulder. There was a gentleness in the way he eyed the other man.

Luis hummed. "I had dealings with the Inquisition before and was wanted by my homeland for crimes on the high seas—I did not want to be caught and sent back to my death. But when Irving explained what they were really doing, I was intrigued. Then we ended up saving Anna from being burned at the stake." He gestured toward the kitchen with his thumb. "I offered to bring them aboard my ship, and we made a short voyage to the Netherlands. I hid my ship, as there was nowhere we could sail without being accosted by other privateers or military vessels, and we made our way on horseback throughout the empire, helping others along the way."

"What an exciting journey you must have had!" Wendell said with a wide grin. His face was lit up and more animated than before. Luis smiled at him. The genuine, soft expression was rare compared to the serious one he often wore. Irving was still staring at Luis with a grin that belied a fondness more intimate than traveling companions. In that moment, Wendell realized the two were in love—the kind of love that surpassed the boundaries of one's homeland and gender. He wanted to ask how it felt to be in love and how they managed to hide it from the world that did not accept or understand them. He thought of Jacques and the kindness he had shown from the beginning, of the friendship that had grown since he awoke from his injuries. Wendell did not have friends to compare his feelings to; the only person who had truly and openly loved him was his grandsire. Still, he thought perhaps this was what love felt like.

"Supper is ready," Jacques announced from the kitchen, startling Wendell from his thoughts. He helped Michael bring in the main dish while Anna set down bowls of vegetables and bread. Steam rose from the pork's flesh, mixing with the aroma of spices; some of which Wendell could not determine. The full table reminded him of not too long ago when his parents and grandfather were sitting in the seats currently occupied by people he never expected to come across. Somehow this group felt more like a family than his own. They talked to him as if they were interested in what he had to say, shared their past with him, and did not recoil about his curse to bring death wherever he went.

Jacques tapped him on the arm, rousing Wendell's attention. "Would you like to say a prayer?" he asked gently.

Wendell glanced around the table, remembering his last conversation with this many people present—insubstantial chatter about a war and the harvest that he did not participate in. He bowed his head, closed his eyes, and laced his fingers together. "Thank you, Lord, for providing sustenance for our bodies. We ask that you continue to watch over us and grant us your mercy. Amen."

"Amen," the table answered. The clinking of cutlery resounded throughout the room.

"You've heard Anna's story already," Irving said as he cut his portion into smaller pieces. "And Luis recounted his days as an outlaw." Luis playfully nudged him with an elbow. "I suppose it is our turn now, Michael." He gestured to his brother, who grunted in response. "Our family has been hunters for generations. We were taught to track down and kill anything deemed 'unnatural' without thinking of the being's humanity."

"Too dangerous," Michael added after swallowing a piece of meat. His voice was gruff and thick from disuse. It surprised Wendell to hear him speak after being accustomed to his silence.

"Yes, it was too dangerous to stop and think about the people behind the horror," Irving said. "But after a while, I no longer wished to hunt that way. I tried to convince my family and fellow huntsmen to find a treatment or a way to coexist with these creatures peacefully but was scoffed at." Irving frowned.

Wendell blinked slowly, a question on the tip of his tongue, tingling. He glanced at Jacques, who met his eyes. They had wondered if others in the world like Wendell—cursed to become a monster—or entities like Nightmare existed without a host. "So, what other kinds of creatures are out there?" he dared to ask.

"We've come across all kinds of beings," Irving stated. "You may have heard tales of a man, who transforms into a wolf under a full moon, called a werewolf. During one hunt, we met with a pack of them. While everyone else loaded their guns with silver bullets, I tried communicating. I was too busy treating them as *people* instead of monsters that I ignored all the warning signs and dangers I had known since birth."

Wendell's eyes widened as Irving spoke, his nostrils flaring slightly. His body tensed as if getting ready to run away.

Irving turned to Michael. "Michael saved me. They were too feral in their transformed state to understand me and attacked. He stepped in the way and got bit instead."

Wendell heard Jacques suck in a breath, staring at Michael as he chewed on another piece of meat. There were no vegetables on his plate, and his portion leaked blood—not as fully cooked as the others' portions. Some juice dribbled from his chin into his beard. Wendell glanced around the table to see everyone's reactions to what Irving said: Anna nibbled on a piece of bread and Luis cut his meat into pieces, both calm at the news. Turning to Jacques, who appeared as alarmed as he felt, they shared a glance.

"Yes," Irving answered the unspoken question, gazing between the two of them. "He became a werewolf himself. We were unable to stop the transformation. My family wanted to kill him. Whenever any of us started to turn, it was considered merciful to kill rather than allow a hunter to become a monster. I snuck him out of our family's prison as quickly as I could."

"Be not afraid, he doesn't bite," Anna grinned, cackling at the nervous expressions Wendell and Jacques gave her.

"That is not funny, Anna," Luis said harshly, though without much bite; almost as if chiding a child. He sighed, turning to Jacques and Wendell. "I know it does not instill the safest thoughts in your mind, but Anna has concocted a potion to keep him in control."

"Wolfsbane," she clarified.

"And he's been working on his awareness while transformed. It's why we believe it could be possible for you to remain in control while you are Nightmare," Irving added. Michael nodded as he chewed.

Wendell tilted his head to the side. "In control?"

"When the wolf takes over, instincts go before logic," Anna

explained, still eating a piece of bread. "He has been practicing control over his instincts while in that form, so he can remember who he is."

"Not perfect, but getting better," Michael said in a gruff voice.

Wendell stared at him and felt his muscles slowly relax as he felt a kindred nature with the other. "You are like me, then." Michael lifted his head up from his food to meet Wendell's eyes and gave a curt nod in agreement.

"So, the other night," Jacques said quietly. "We heard a sound like a wolf's howl. The moon was full and sky clear. Was that . . . you?" He stared at Michael in awe.

"Indeed," Irving answered for him. He had his fingers laced together, glancing between Jacques and Wendell as if measuring their reactions. "You heard Michael's howl that night."

# 17

# The Crucial Experiments

After the meal, Anna took out instruments from her bag and laid them out on the cleared table. One was a long tube connected to a needle and a vial. She showed it to Wendell. "I'm going to use this to take some of your blood." She made a small cut into his skin. He winced, hissing as she pressed the vial underneath allowing the blood to flow out of him and into the container. She then applied deeper pressure to stem the bleeding and wrapped a bandage around the cut tightly. It left him a bit dizzy. She gave him water to drink and something to snack on. He watched as she took out more cylindrical tubes and vials containing different colored liquids. Anna let a few drops of his blood go into an empty vial, then poured one of the clear liquids into it. She swirled the contents together and stared at them thoughtfully. Wendell craned his neck to see what she was doing, and only noticed the color darken somewhat.

Anna's face scrunched up at the result, and she repeated the process with different combinations from her vials and placed the containers atop a heating device to make them boil. She was oddly silent throughout the process, occasionally muttering to herself but otherwise completely absorbed in her task. She ran her hands through her hair several times until she tied it up into a lopsided ponytail with a few stray hairs sticking out. Once they had boiled, she took out a magnifying glass to examine the liquids.

"Any findings?" Irving asked as he approached them.

She shook her head, still staring at the samples.

"The other villagers have been asking about our progress. Father Heinrich keeps warning me that if we can't undo the curse before the new moon, we'll be in danger," Irving told her.

Luis snorted. "In danger of becoming the next sacrifice, you mean?"

"I've been wondering about that, actually," Irving said, turning to Wendell. "How is it done?"

Wendell frowned, pressing his lips into a thin line. "It's not like someone is bound at an altar to be devoured," he explained. "It's just . . . like fate. Sometimes the crops spoil before harvest time, sometimes a sickness overcomes a healthy person." He glanced at Jacques as he continued, his face pale. "And sometimes, a lost traveler wanders in at the wrong time."

There was only the sound of boiling liquid in the room. He took a deep breath. "My first transformation was the worst," he began. "It was painful, and at some point, I think I lost consciousness; or I simply cannot remember the rest." He closed his eyes for a moment. "We weren't sure when it would begin—the first time usually occurs between childhood and adulthood, so the village wasn't prepared that night. I had just woken up and felt compelled to go to the forest but was unsure why. Then it happened." Wendell paused, taking a shuddering breath. Jacques reached out to him, placing a hand on his shoulder in comfort. "The next morning, they said, Grandfather told me, there was a boy—little Wilhelm. He was found," Wendell's hands dug into his thighs, "he was found outside, dead. I was lying beside him, covered in . . . covered in his blood." He buried his face in his hands as tears slid down his puffy cheeks.

Jacques' face tightened with shock, and then he pulled Wendell closer, holding him as he cried. Anna finally stepped away from her experiments and reached out to Wendell, placing a gentle hand on his back. Luis averted his eyes; his expression unreadable. Irving and Michael had matching expressions of stoic empathy. They shared a knowing gaze.

Michael stepped forward, kneeling in front of Wendell. "It wasn't your fault."

Irving leaned forward to gently add, "It never is."

"You didn't choose to be this way," Luis said in a soft tone. "Which is why we're here to help you. Your grandfather," he paused as Wendell turned to him, "he told us how kind you were, and how much you blame yourself for what happened. His greatest wish was to see you happy and free from the burden of this curse."

Wendell sniffed, wiping the wetness from his face. "He was my only friend here," he said. "I just want to make this stop. I don't want to kill anymore."

"We'll find a way to break this curse," Irving stated, eyes focused.

## LAST QUARTER MOON

"You have to try harder," Luis commanded, watching Wendell struggle with a stern gaze. Throughout the following days, Wendell tried to summon Nightmare and control the transformation, with no luck. They stood in the backyard of Wendell's home, hidden from view by anyone walking down the path, as Wendell tried to connect with the beast inside of him. Despite the cool air, Wendell felt himself sweat with exertion as he attempted to find Nightmare's presence and convince it to appear.

"I'm doing my best," Wendell gasped, squeezing his eyes shut.

"Your best isn't good enough." Luis had his hand on his hip, scowling at Wendell in disappointment.

"Luis, don't be too hard on him," Irving ordered with a frown. His partner rolled his eyes and sighed.

"You're doing great, Wendell," Jacques whispered reassuringly beside him.

"No, nothing's happening. I just can't get it," Wendell muttered.

"I told you; it has to do with the right attitude," Luis commented.

"Perhaps we're doing something wrong. Let's try other ways," Irving said with a hand to his chin.

"Like what? Try to scare him into transforming?" Luis replied. Jacques glared directly at Luis, who met his stare evenly.

Irving glanced at Wendell, who was terrified, and muttered, "Maybe there's some other kind of stimulation we can find."

"How did you learn to control it?" Wendell asked Michael.

The werewolf was quiet for a moment. "Having hunted for so long, I thought I knew my enemy; knew what it was like to be something other than human," he began, speaking slowly and struggling to get words out at times. "But I was wrong. Irving was the one who really understood it. He saw them as people who needed help, not as animals needing to be put down."

Wendell nodded, listening with understanding eyes.

"It was he who taught me how to tame the wolf," Michael continued. "He was patient, but firm. The first few times, I blacked out and could not remember anything. When he told me I killed people, I was sick with the knowledge that I had become the kind of monster I once hunted. But he didn't turn on me."

"Were you that close as brothers, that he loved you too much to kill you?" Wendell asked. He thought of his grandfather, who had always stood up for him against his own parents and the villagers.

Michael shook his head. "It was not familial ties that kept me alive. As soon as our parents discovered I had been bitten, they tried to kill me. We had to flee."

"Ah," Wendell replied, nodding again.

"I assume your parents weren't fond of you because you were born the Nightmare's vessel," Irving said gently.

"They . . ." Wendell paused, choosing his words carefully. "They were burdened with a child they could not love."

Michael frowned. "A parent who cannot love their child is more a monster than someone like us."

"I understood their fear and hatred of me. I never could hold it against them," Wendell explained. "It hurt, yes, but everyone treated me like that—except Grandfather. He was the only one who saw me as Wendell, not Nightmare."

Michael nodded. "Irving was the same. He refused to treat me differently. Just changed his approach when it came to my other side. He helped me keep control during transformations, kept reminding me of who I was, but never blamed me."

"I'm glad more people like my grandfather are out there. I always thought he was the odd one for the way he treated me so kindly. Sometimes I thought it was wrong."

"You were taught to believe *you* were evil, not just Nightmare," Luis stated.

Wendell swallowed a hard lump in his throat at the painful truth. "Yes, the villagers couldn't separate the person from the curse. I only wish they had, because then we could have found a way to subdue it."

"You still have work to do when it comes to your transformations. Jacques will be your partner." Irving said, nodding toward Jacques. "The two of you share a bond similar to Michael and me. He could be the one to bring balance."

Wendell felt a blush come upon him at Irving's words. "He's never treated me like a monster. Even after what I did to him."

Irving put a hand on his shoulder. "You can't let that haunt you," he said softly.

Wendell shook his head. "It's not just him. I've killed people as Nightmare."

"Use those incidents as a reminder of what could happen should you lose control over Nightmare," Irving suggested. "That may help you maintain composure."

# 18

# The Hidden Monster

## NEW MOON

**After much discussion, the group** agreed to oversee Wendell's transformation so they could glean information about Nightmare. Jacques tentatively consented to attempt a conversation with the creature as Albrecht had done. The sky began to darken. Wendell opened the door and stepped out onto the porch. Jacques stood beside him. Windows and doors closed loudly throughout the village; latches and locks were being secured by the occupants. No one was out on the road and the air was still.

"Are you sure?" Wendell asked Jacques softly.

Jacques took a deep breath, forcing his limbs to relax. He couldn't stop his heart from pounding fiercely within his chest. "Yes," he breathed, hoping he sounded more confident than he felt.

"We'll be there with you," Irving stated, emerging from the home. "If something goes wrong, I promise to get you out of there safely." Jacques nodded at him, noticing the pistol sheathed at the Hunter's side. Luis held a shotgun and was tucking knives into various pockets in his pants. "It's just a precaution," Irving said, noticing Jacques staring at their weapons. "We have no intention of hurting Wendell, but other threats may be out there."

"I mixed together a few tonics that might help us tonight," Anna told them, handing out one to each of them except for Wendell. "Drink this if you begin feeling weak or ill based on the curse's influence. Remember not to get too close to it."

"I don't know how Nightmare will react," Wendell admitted. "He may become hostile. Please don't let me hurt any of you."

"It wouldn't be you, Wendell," Irving told him.

Wendell dipped his head and swallowed, tucking some hair behind his ear. The front steps creaked as he walked down onto the path leading to the forest. The others followed silently, only the crunch of their boots on the ground. Fresh snow had fallen during the day, covering up the roadways. Wendell guided the group to the tree line while the sun lowered in the sky. The further they went into the dense woodland, the more limited their vision became. Light did not shine through the trees and the underbrush was covered in snow, making it difficult to avoid roots and limbs hiding beneath the ground. It got too dark in front of them. Irving lit a torch. Once Wendell reached a clearing, Jacques and the hunters hid behind bushes and thick trees, waiting for the transformation.

Clouds parted the sky, revealing the moon barely visible against the darkness. Wendell's breathing quickened and he winced in pain as small, round bumps formed, poking through his blond hair. Blood dripped from the protrusions as they grew taller, taking on the shape of antlers.

The group watched as Wendell's bones began to bend in unusual shapes, and the cracking and snapping made Anna startle slightly. Wendell cried out, falling to his hands and knees as his legs elongated, the skin stretching and tearing. His arms were shaking as they changed into forelegs, while his fingers joined together to form hooves. Tears were streaming down Wendell's bloody face as his jaw unhinged, revealing sharp fangs amongst blunt teeth. His clothes ripped at the strain, revealing tufts of fur covered in gore and boney ribs poking through. Hot breath coalescing with the cold air created a mist around him, and his voice took on a more animalistic tone.

As Nightmare emerged from the young man's form, it steadied itself, long ears twitching to flick off excess residue. It shook its whole body, flinging blood onto the ground, which hissed and melted. Its eyes, the only thing still resembling Wendell, took in the area.

Seeing the form that had haunted his sleep for so long again gave Jacques a jolt. He trembled and absently clutched at his injured arm, as if the limb could remember the pain of being impaled upon the points of antlers. His breath came out quickly, creating a mist in the air and sounding too loud in the darkness.

Beside him, Anna scribbled hurriedly in her notebook throughout the process, sketching out the creature in front of them and taking notes. She whispered to herself while she wrote. Nightmare's head turned in her direction. Jacques sucked in a breath, worried the beast would go after her if Wendell were unable to control it. Trepidation sank deep into his bones as he began to regret such a dangerous feat.

Jacques noticed that Irving kept his hand near his pistol, staring at the beast intensely as it sniffed the air. A noise in the distance drew its attention for a moment; Luis cocking the shotgun. The distinct feeling of an overwhelming presence filled the clearing, making tiny hairs stick up on his arms and neck. Nightmare snorted and turned to stare in the direction where Jacques crouched, as if waiting for him to come out.

Jacques glanced at Irving, who nodded at him before returning his gaze to the monster. Filled with fear, Jacques stood slowly and walked closer. A rotting smell invaded his nose as he approached. The ground beneath the creature's hooves was dark and barren. Licking his cracked lips, Jacques took a deep breath.

"My name is Jacques. You attacked me the last time we met; do you remember?" he asked.

Nightmare slowly blinked at him—a gesture that reminded him so much of Wendell that it unnerved him. Thick red drool dropped onto the ground from its maw.

Jacques felt his muscles tightening and releasing, unable to calm his ragged breathing. "Can you understand me?" he tried again. Nightmare took a step toward him and he jerked back. He told himself to remain steady and clenched his fists. "Wendell, do you hear me?" Despite the lack of response, he could feel a strange connection with the creature. Something in his mind told him that the beast knew who he was—not as Wendell, but as Nightmare. Something didn't feel right in his gut, and a sharp pain filled his head.

Suddenly, Nightmare stomped on the ground and unleashed a loud grunt. Irving called out to Jacques, drawing his pistol. A shotgun bullet hit a nearby tree in an attempt to warn the creature away. Nightmare let out a roar of anger, sending a shiver down Jacques' spine. It turned, charging toward the source of the gunfire. Irving shot at the area around it to draw it away. Nightmare wheeled around and reared up on its hind legs. Jacques saw Irving's legs tremble as the buck started charging him instead.

Jacques gasped and dove out of the way, losing control of his actions. He was running again, just like before. As shotguns and pistols rang out in the dense forest behind him, he clapped his hands to his ears. His vision narrowed, darkness encroaching on the edges. He kept running, chest aching and lungs choking on the cold air. Stumbling on a large branch, he skidded forward to land on his hands and knees. Scrambling to stand, he ripped at the earth and kicked dirt up.

In the distance, he heard Anna shriek. Jacques stopped, clinging to a tree. As the blood pumped in his ears, faint sounds grew louder.

"Over there!" Irving's distinct voice cut through the haze.

"Watch the points, it's rearing again!" Luis yelled. The shotgun went off and Jacques flinched.

He was breathing heavily, blinking away the blurriness as his nerves began to steady. "I have to go back," he told himself. But his body didn't move, stuck and shaking against the tree trunk he clung to. "I have to help them!" He told himself, willing his arms and legs to move, trying to overcome the intense feeling of fear and dread threatening to choke him.

Turning around, he ran toward the clearing to see the hunters surrounding Nightmare, keeping their distance. It charged at one and then another, angling its antlers to skewer whoever got in its path. The hunters called out from either side, shooting their guns in the air while Anna threw sticks and other debris to distract the creature. It almost worked. Jacques reappeared at the edge of the clearing.

"Jacques, get to safety!" Irving commanded.

"We're not here to hurt you!" Jacques ignored him and yelled out, stepping closer to Nightmare.

A rush of heat and the pungent scent of decay pushed him back, singeing the ground and darkening the closest trees. Luis coughed, covering his mouth, and stumbled backward.

"Drink the potion!" Anna shouted before taking a sip.

Jacques watched as Luis fumbled with the bottle in his hand while holding the shotgun with his other. Nightmare homed in on him, huffing and raking the ground with its hoof. "Wendell, stop!" Jacques yelled. It ignored him, rushing toward Luis.

"Michael, now!" Irving shouted.

A tall figure stepped forward from behind the trees, letting out an aggressive growl in warning to the other predator. In the dim light, Jacques saw that it was covered in thick fur and stood on two elongated legs. Long, sharp claws on paw-like hands curled like it was about to strike. The head resembled a wolf, its frightening fangs bared in warning at Nightmare, which reacted to this new threat by slowing to stalk toward the werewolf.

As the beasts faced off, Irving grabbed hold of Jacques and dragged him back behind the tree line. "Stay by me," he whispered. They went deeper into the forest and crouched down, watching. Anna quickly join them with Luis, who plopped down unsteadily. Irving reached out to him with concern showing plainly on his face. "Are you all right?"

"I'm fine," Luis wheezed, sweat slicking his skin and seeping through his tunic.

"He drank the potion. It should make him better soon," Anna reassured Irving.

A familiar roar made Jacques' head whip around to watch the werewolf lunge at Nightmare. Claws raked through fur while teeth snapped ferociously. Nightmare reared back, shaking the werewolf off. Its antlers pointed down as it charged forward. The werewolf barely avoided being impaled and rushed around to the buck's flank, whose hind legs kicked out with a well-aimed strike. The werewolf was thrown to the ground a few feet away and whimpered. A dark imprint of hooves formed on its belly. As the werewolf got up, some of its fur dropped to the ground.

"He'll die!" Jacques cried, grabbing at Irving's arm. "We have to stop them!"

"Michael can hold his own in this form," Irving replied. His tone sounded like he was trying to convince himself just as much as Jacques.

Jacques pointed to the darkened area on the werewolf's stomach. "It doesn't matter how strong he is, he's been touched by death!"

"We don't know how other supernatural creatures are affected. This could be a chance to learn something new," Anna said, still writing in her notebook feverishly.

"I don't like it," Luis said. He turned to Irving. "I felt sick and nearly fainted being near that thing. If Michael is directly hit, he could already be dying."

Irving stared at the monsters as they tore at each other, knocking over trees and letting out horrendous sounds. The ground was torn up at their feet and birds scattered into the sky, cawing out in fear. "No way to stop them now; the werewolf is engaged with another predator and his instincts have taken over. He'll likely attack us if we try to interfere."

"What about Wendell?" Jacques snapped. "I thought you said you weren't going to hurt him."

"This was the backup plan if Nightmare attacked while you spoke with it. I hoped it wouldn't get this far," Irving told him. He squinted in thought. "I think it knew what we were doing—it's retaliating against our interference."

"I have to admit, the two of them fighting is awe-inspiring," Anna said, watching with wide eyes. Luis nudged her, shaking his head.

"It's terrifying!" Jacques shouted in panic.

"Michael's transformation is only temporary when not under a full moon," Irving said. "We can rescue him once he turns back."

Jacques shook his head vigorously. "You don't understand, Nightmare will kill him and then come for all of us next. This was a bad idea, just like Wendell said!"

"If we didn't take any risks, we would never be able to learn so much about these beings. Trust me," Irving told him. "I know you're worried and scared, but we *do* have a plan."

"We didn't want to tell you or Wendell, in case Nightmare found out," Anna explained quickly.

Before Jacques could respond, Luis stood abruptly. "Michael is changing back."

"Give the signal," Irving ordered. "Luis, are you able to go on?"

"Of course I am," Luis said, already heading toward the sounds of carnage. Irving followed him as Anna gave out a high-pitched whistle. She did it a few times before a return whistle was heard from nearby. She indicated Jacques to come with her as they snuck through the woods.

They met up with a man leading a lamb with a rope. "Release it," Anna told him. The man nodded and urged the animal forward with a smack to his rump before running back toward the village. It brayed, bolting into the woods. They listened as the sounds of violence died out, replaced with the screams of the lamb. The bushes in front of them rustled, startling Jacques. Something heavy was being dragged through the bushes and he tensed, unsure whether he should run or fight. Irving and Luis appeared, carrying Michael. He was wounded and unconscious, covered in blood and bruises. Jacques relaxed slowly, unsure if they were truly out of danger just yet.

"He's alive," Irving said in a relieved breath. "It's time to head back."

Jacques took the place of Luis, who loaded another bullet into his shotgun while they hurried through the woods. Jacques was unsure if they would ever find their way out until he saw the village in the distance. They emerged from the forest where the man from before waited with Father Heinrich, Doctor Obstein, and Katharina.

"You people are mad," the man exclaimed upon seeing Michael.

"Nightmare got its sacrifice," Irving told them.

"Hopefully you have not angered it, or God, with your actions tonight," the clergyman snapped.

"We may have riled it up, but we learned a lot more about it," Anna said, waving her notebook.

"I'll take care of him," Obstein stated, gesturing toward Michael. "Katharina, go ahead of us to prepare."

"Yes, Doctor," the midwife said, rushing toward the apothecary.

"Do you think he'll die from his wounds?" Jacques asked the doctor quietly. He warily eyed the hoof-shaped bruises on Michael's stomach, which already showed signs of decay.

"I am unsure, but have been made aware of his condition," the doctor replied. "We can only hope that being abnormal will weaken the effects."

Jacques turned his gaze back toward the woods where silence had fallen.

# 19

# The Dire Consequences

## WAXING CRESCENT MOON

**A**t dawn, Jacques was awoken by the creaking of steps. He sat up from his spot in the chair he had placed near the door as it opened, revealing Wendell stumbling in wearing the torn-up clothes from the night before and covered in dirt. His mouth was bloody and his hair was disheveled. Jacques rushed forward, catching him as he almost fell.

"What happened?" Wendell asked weakly, collapsing into Jacques' embrace.

"Nightmare wouldn't talk to me," Jacques replied, guiding Wendell to the couch. "It tried to attack us."

Wendell stirred against him, eyes wide and wild. "Did I hurt anyone?" he gasped out.

"Michael turned into the werewolf and fought Nightmare so we could get away. He was wounded but still alive, so they took him to the apothecary. Irving stayed with him last night. Anna and Luis went back to the inn; they seemed to be unharmed."

Wendell reached behind himself and touched his back. "That would explain these." Jacques peered around him to see thick, deep gashes along Wendell's back. They weren't bleeding, though dried flakes were scattered across his skin. At Jacques' alarmed expression, Wendell told him, "Most wounds Nightmare sustains can heal." He winced. "These hurt, I'll have to see Doctor Obstein, but I should be okay. However," he turned sad eyes to Jacques. "Michael will die if Nightmare touched him."

Jacques sighed, feeling himself tear up at the thought of losing someone he just met. "I told them that. I wanted to be here when you returned, so I don't know if he's still alive. We should take you over there right away." He helped Wendell up and wrapped a blanket around him.

"I can't forgive myself if—"

Jacques shook his head. "We can't think like that. Maybe he'll be able to heal, too."

"I don't know, Jacques. I don't . . ." Wendell was shaking his head frantically. His skin felt cold to Jacques, who lead him outside. Walking down the path, Jacques noticed doors and windows were being unlatched. Faces peered out at them from small openings. Their expressions reminded him of vultures waiting for predators to leave their prey. He brushed off some of the dirt in Wendell's hair and Wendell leaned closer into him.

Doctor Obstein was washing his hands at the water pump outside of the apothecary as they approached. He lifted his head; mouth set in a grim line. "Here we are again, Wendell. Yet another body lays on my table after encountering Nightmare."

"I'm so sorry, I," Wendell sobbed, reaching out to the doctor.

Obstein clutched Wendell's shoulders tightly, holding his gaze. "Calm yourself! I will not have you disturbing the man from his rest."

"He's upset, and his back—" Jacques began to explain, pulling

Wendell toward him.

"I know, son," Obstein said to him in a softer tone. "This is not the first time, nor will it be the last." He turned back to Wendell. "But you must keep yourself together, Wendell. Remember what I told you: breathe and think not of the past."

Wendell took heaving breaths, grasping at his arms. Jacques watched quietly for a moment and then dug into his pocket where he had placed the small jar Anna gave to Wendell. Wendell had asked Jacques to bring it with him when they went into the woods the night before, in case he had another episode.

"Here," Jacques handed the jar to Wendell, who opened it and inhaled the scent of the herbs. His shaking hands began to ease into stillness as Wendell kept breathing in deep and slow. The ragged noise evened out and Wendell closed his eyes.

"What is this?" Obstein indicated the jar.

"Anna made it to help him calm down," Jacques explained.

Obstein raised his eyebrows. "Well, it seems like she had the right ingredients. I've made tonics for him, but they never worked the same as for others with such a nervous and excitable disposition. I'll have to ask her what she used."

"Can we go in now?" Wendell asked in a calm voice. He was visibly relaxed and tears had begun to dry on his face.

Obstein nodded his head and opened the door. "They're sleeping, please be quiet."

Irving was crumpled in a chair next to the table where Michael was laid with a blanket draped over him. His face was turned to the side, eyes closed.

"He stayed awake well past the time it took to tend to his brother's wounds," Obstein whispered.

Luis emerged with a cup of tea in hand, pausing when he noticed Jacques and Wendell. He held a finger to his lips and stood next to Irving, eyes intent on him.

Wendell approached the table. Michael was bandaged around his midsection, with a few visible cuts and bruises on his arms. His legs were covered with a blanket and his chest rose and fell steadily. Jacques stood beside Wendell, staring at Michael in awe.

"Evidently werewolves have strong healing capabilities," Luis murmured in explanation.

"Yes, astounding really," Obstein said softly. "The only wound we are unsure of is this one," he said, gesturing to the man's stomach. "I speculate he may have internal damage, perhaps decaying organs. I have seen it before, but those were during my analysis of the dead."

"Anna will most likely want to perform some tests," Luis replied with a sigh. "Whenever she wakes up," he grumbled. He lowered his gaze to Irving, placing a hand on his shoulder.

Wendell slowly extended his hand over Michael's stomach, inspecting the bandages. No blood seeped through, but he could see dark shapes through the linen. Gingerly, he lowered his hand until he was just barely touching the center of the wound. Jacques and Obstein stared in silence, Jacques not daring to breathe. Wendell let out a deep breath and closed his eyes.

"Dear Lord," he whispered. "Please heal this man from the wounds inflicted by Nightmare. I repent of my sins and ask for your forgiveness. Punish me for my misdeeds but spare this man his life." Wendell opened his eyes and raised his hand.

"Do you really think that will work?" Luis asked, gazing at Wendell in doubt.

Wendell's mouth turned down. "It's all I know to do besides what Doctor Obstein has already done. If I am the curse meant to atone for the sins of the village, then perhaps God will spare him and allow me to take the pain instead." He met Jacques' eyes. "I prayed over you as well. I like to think He heard me, and that's why you woke up."

"Father Heinrich may have better knowledge of that, though I am unsure if we should tell him about this," Obstein said, patting Wendell on the back.

Luis's eyes softened as he observed Wendell and he let out a hum, ruffling his hair. He sat down on a nearby chair, finally taking a sip of his tea. "You're too nice for this kind of life, kid."

Obstein regarded Wendell fondly, nodding his head in agreement. "I am glad others are starting to realize this. If only the rest of this village could see what we do."

Wendell gave Luis and the doctor a small smile, ducking his head. He was unused to so much affection and praise.

The door burst open as Anna ran in, hair frizzled and unkempt. "I had an epiphany!"

"Shush, woman!" Obstein hissed.

Anna ducked her head and slapped a hand to her mouth.

Luis cursed in Spanish, having jumped and spilled tea on himself at her entrance. Irving roused, bleary eyes taking in everyone around him. The blanket fell from his shoulders and onto his lap as he sat up.

She came forward to check on Michael, who was still asleep.

"How is he?" Irving asked, standing and smoothing down the wrinkles on his shirt. He ran his hands through his mussed-up hair to comb it out.

"Still asleep, surprisingly," Luis muttered, dabbing at his wet shirt with a cloth. "The doctor has been keeping an eye on him for you."

Irving stared at Obstein expectantly. "The man is alive and steady," the doctor replied. "From what I've seen, he should heal rather quickly."

"And the curse's effect?" Irving asked. He glanced between Wendell and Obstein.

Obstein crossed his arms over his chest. "I am unsure how he will fare, being what he is."

"That's what my epiphany was about," Anna said, stepping closer. "Werewolves heal faster than humans, and can survive fatal wounds—"

"Yes, we know that Anna," Irving interrupted impatiently.

"And vampires are immortal," Anna continued as if Irving hadn't spoken.

"Vampires?" Jacques asked with raised eyebrows. Luis shook his head at him to indicate that this was not the time to ask about it.

Irving rolled his eyes and gestured for her to keep going. Anna was motioning with her whole body frantically. "*Immortal*, Irving!" she emphasized. "Like most of the creatures we've seen. They either heal quickly—if they sustain injuries at all—or are long-lived. Do you see?" She clapped Jacques on the back. "He could be too. That's why he survived his encounter with Nightmare! Maybe this curse of death only affects humans—*mortals*!"

Stunned, Jacques glanced between them. A hint of understanding crossed over Irving's face, and he turned to Jacques. "She could be right," he said in awe.

Obstein's eyebrows came together. "You are referring to beings that are impervious to death," he stated. The doctor indicated Jacques knowingly. "In all my medical research and scientific studies, I have never come across this kind of information. Yet I believe you may be right."

"That's because it isn't discussed publicly," Irving said, pacing with his hand at his chin. "The knowledge of such beings is mostly passed on to the hunters who deal them; much like this village, which has prevented word of the curse from getting outside, countless other places have done the same."

"But it's widely known within those communities that some of these creatures exist for an indefinite amount of time," Anna added. "Immortality. Humans have been searching for the ability to live forever while maintaining their youth for centuries; when all they really need to do is become a shapeshifter!"

Luis snorted. "I'd prefer the world not be overrun by them."

Jacques carded his hand through his hair. "This is all a bit much to take in so quickly, I'm afraid." He was shaking his head, trying to clear it from all the nonsense the hunters were saying. It was just like when Albrecht and Wendell explained the curse to him the first time. He felt overwhelmed with information he could not comprehend and didn't have the proper amount of time to process.

"Is it really so hard to imagine yourself immortal?" Irving asked.

Jacques thought back to his conversation with Obstein about the bullet wound on his chest—the one that supposedly went straight through his heart. "Well," he started and checked with Obstein, who gave a slight nod. "Not exactly." The eyes of everyone were upon him. He sighed. "I've had other close encounters before; but I was just lucky." He hugged his arms around himself. "Though if you're right, I guess that makes sense."

Wendell was staring at him strangely, as if seeing him fully and understanding something that could not be named.

"Yes! That would explain why you survived," Anna said excitedly.

"In order to uphold your theory, Michael would have to pull through as well," Luis pointed out. "Right now, we have to wait."

"Oh, I'm sure he'll wake up in no time!" Anna said cheerily. She always remained happily optimistic, no matter the situation.

"He was struck full on, Anna. I doubt he'll be able to fully heal even with his abilities," Luis retorted, ever the pessimist.

While the two argued over the state of their friend's health, Irving stared at Jacques, who avoided his gaze. After a moment, the hunter turned to the doctor, who met his eye. A silent conversation seemed to happen between them. Wendell tugged on Jacques' shirt, indicating for them to go outside.

"Is something wrong?" Wendell asked quietly.

Jacques shifted in place. "No, I don't know how to explain it."

"About your past and where you came from? I don't even know that about you, Jacques."

Jacques pursed his lips. "I am from Lorraine and was traveling through the area to explore the world. What else do you need to know?" He gave Wendell a grin, but the other seemed unconvinced.

"I understand if there are things you wish not to tell," Wendell said, lowering his head. "We all have our secrets." He absently played with his hair, something Jacques noticed he did when he was nervous or uncomfortable.

Jacques shuffled his feet. "We live in a time of war, Wendell. People are dying for what they believe in, just like Luis' family. Sometimes keeping a secret could mean life or death."

Wendell nodded his head. "I know," he said, as if bearing such a secret himself. He touched Jacques' hand. "But I hope to one day earn your trust to share in that secret. Who am I to judge your beliefs or doings?"

Jacques gave him a soft smile. "It is not you I worry about knowing, but the others; especially in this village. Your parents," he stopped, swallowing. "I think they would have hurled me down the steps if they knew."

Wendell's eyes hardened and his grip tightened on Jacques' hand. "I will not allow *anyone* to hurt you," he said fiercely. It reminded Jacques of the first time the Inquisitors came, bringing on Wendell's wrath.

"So, you promise to protect me as well?"

Wendell's expression softened and he smiled fully. "Yes."

A crowd had formed outside of the apothecary. They stood silently in their ritual cloaks, masks in hand. Wendell watched through the window as Father Heinrich parted the crowd to knock on the door.

The doctor opened it and stepped outside, closing it behind him. His words were easy for Wendell to hear from inside. "You may all go home. The Inquisitors were not the sacrifice last night."

Wendell saw the priest frown briefly, and then smile wide. "What wonderful news! Let us rejoice in their survival."

"Who, then?" a woman in the crowd asked, gripping her mask tightly. "I heard gunshots in the dead of night and screams from the woods. Who was slain?" The gathered villagers glanced around at each other as if searching for whoever might be missing.

Doctor Obstein raised his hands to calm the restless crowd as they shifted and murmured at her words. "No one died. We brought an offering, and it was accepted."

"God be praised!" Father Heinrich exclaimed, raising his hands in the air. "Then we must congratulate them on their accomplishment." He took a step toward the door, but Obstein did not move away to let him through.

"I must ask that you wait. One of them was wounded and requires my care and some rest," the doctor told him.

"Then allow me to offer a blessing and our thanks," Father Heinrich insisted.

Obstein hesitated before allowing the clergyman to step past him. The villagers waited behind him as the door closed.

The group watched the arrival of the priest. Wendell instinctively stepped behind Jacques, peering around him.

"What in God's name were you people doing last night?" Father Heinrich hissed. "Causing a ruckus and terrifying the whole town, were you trying to kill the thing?" He peered around the room. "Well, where is he? Where is Wendell?"

Obstein held out a hand. "Calm yourself, Father," he said.

Irving stepped forward with a stern expression. "We were trying to communicate with it," he stated.

Father Heinrich drew back, appalled. "And why ever would you do such a thing?" he asked.

"To better understand it," Irving responded. "We want to find a remedy so your village no longer suffers under this curse and to ensure it won't spread to others."

The clergyman visibly relaxed, exhaling deeply and placing a hand over his chest. "Yes, yes, of course." He rubbed his hands together, eyes going elsewhere. "We have faith in you to rid us of this madness." Noticing Michael laying on the table behind Irving and Luis, he said, "And to think one of you was wounded in the task." His change of tone was drastic as he bowed. "My sincerest apologies. Please allow me to pray for his recovery."

Luis and Irving met eyes before moving aside. Father Heinrich took out prayer beads from beneath his robes, clutching them in his hands. "Oh Lord, place Your hands upon the afflicted and lift his ailments. Release him of the pain he is suffering from and let him feel Your healing touch. Amen." He made the sign of the cross over Michael's wound.

"Thank you," Obstein said. "I am sure God will grant him the ability to recover."

Father Heinrich gave a small bow. "I am, humbly, at your service. And please do come to the church while you are here. All are welcome in God's House." He smiled, nodded at each of them, and then took his leave.

"Well, that was strange," Anna said as soon as the priest was gone.

Jacques swiveled around to Wendell. "Why do you think he was so upset?" he asked.

Wendell simply shook his head. "He scares me," he admitted, stepping to the side of Jacques. He reached for the other's arm, grasping it tightly.

"I cannot say as to what the man is thinking, though I admit he has been acting rather odd since you all showed up," Obstein said.

"He is not the first zealous religious leader we have dealt with," Luis murmured.

"Doctor, you say he's been acting odd, how so?" Irving asked, eyebrows coming together.

"His interest in you and your work is uncommon for him," Obstein replied. "Although, you are the first Inquisitors who have openly entered this village, perhaps he wishes to get to know more about your methods and ethics, as a man of God."

"His treatment of Wendell appears the same as the others," Anna said, walking over to pat his shoulder reassuringly. "Shame, someone like him should be the most eager to reach out to those in need of Godly intervention."

Wendell shook his head. "I was never welcomed at the church. Grandfather had to bring home the lessons for me to learn."

"Yes, those born with the curse are forbidden from participating in most activities, in fear of it influencing the next afflicted family," Obstein explained. "The Uhrmachers were doubly cursed upon coming to this village."

# 20

# The Strange Conversation

### WAXING CRESCENT

**Jacques stared at the ceiling,** unable to fall asleep. Memories of his encounters with Nightmare haunted him; from the first time he saw the beast to watching Wendell become it. Until they observed the transformation, he could keep the two separate in his mind. Now, however, he could not see one without the other. He also thought about his moment of panic when he ran away from the clearing. As though he would never stop running. *Am I a coward?* he asked himself, frowning.

He fled from the battlefield and into this village. He would have kept going if not for meeting Wendell; would have been much farther away by this time. His legs twitched, ready to take flight even now, with Wendell asleep nearby him. *How can I protect him if I can't face anything without fleeing?*

As he rubbed his eyes, he heard Wendell stir. Turning, he saw the other go still while his breathing became harsh. Goosebumps appeared on Jacques' body and his chest tightened.

"Wendy?" he whispered.

*"He is asleep,"* a deep voice responded with a tinny dissonance as if several people were talking at once.

Jacques felt a cold sweat run down his back and froze with fear. Wendell remained rigid in sleep, hands by his sides, but his eyes were wide open. "Is this . . . Nightmare?" he asked tentatively.

*"Yes,"* Wendell's mouth moved in response.

Jacques gasped and sat up, clambering away.

*"You wished to speak with me. Why do you run at the sound of my voice?"* Nightmare asked.

It was unsettling how different the creature sounded from Wendell's soft, timid voice, despite speaking through his lips. Jacques glanced away, unable to relax. His mind raced, trying to make sense of what was happening.

"You did not respond last time," Jacques said.

*"I could not,"* Nightmare replied. Jacques was shaking, unable to look at his friend. He opened his mouth to respond, but nothing came out. He did not know what to say now that the creature was finally talking to him. *"I can smell your fear, human. My antlers have been stained with your blood, and yet you live. Do you want to know why?"*

Sucking in a breath, Jacques slowly turned. "You know?"

*"Yes,"* it responded. *"Death knows all."*

"Are you a form of death?" Jacques breathed shakily.

*"I am. It was your people who made me this way."*

Blinking, Jacques was stunned. "My people?"

*"Do you want to know why you cannot die, Jacques le Lorrain?"*

Jacques crawled closer, leaning over Wendell whose eyes remained fixed on the ceiling. "Tell me . . . please," he said.

*"You are not a mortal man."* Wendell's eyes suddenly focused directly on Jacques, who was startled and fell back, cursing loudly.

Wendell blinked, moving his arms to sit up. "Jacques? What happened?" he asked, concerned.

After Jacques haltingly told Wendell about the conversation with Nightmare, they decided to inform the hunters.

"It was eerie; the voice did not sound like Wendy at all," Jacques explained with a shudder.

"Fascinating, so the creature *can* speak," Obstein noted.

Irving was sitting by Michael's bedside, reading the other notes Doctor Obstein made about the curse. When he heard movement from the table, he jumped up to see his brother's eyes open. Wendell and Jacques stepped closer as the doctor approached the bed from the other side to assist his patient.

"How are you feeling?" Irving asked. Michael grunted, sitting up slowly. He touched his chest, which Obstein put a stethoscope to. "The doctor patched you up as well as he could," Irving explained at Michael's confusion.

"The wound," Michael said, pressing down.

"Doctor," Irving said. "Let's remove the bandages."

"Yes, let us check the marks."

Irving nodded. They undid the wrappings to see the imprint of the hoofmarks on freshly grown skin that was darker than the rest of Michael's body. To anyone else, it would have appeared to be a large birthmark. Wendell gasped when he saw the visual representation of his curse manifested on someone else. Jacques' face paled.

"Astounding," Obstein said in awe.

Michael gave Irving a look of bewilderment. "Doesn't hurt," he remarked.

"Anna will be thrilled," Irving said drily. "Her theory seems to be proven. I'm just glad you're alive." He clapped his brother on the back and gave him a warm smile.

Michael gave a huff of agreement and then studied Wendell

with concern.

Wendell approached the bed with a watery expression, relieved and in awe at seeing Michael alive—two people had survived the curse thus far. It felt like a miracle. "I am fine. There were a few scratches on my back from the fight, but Anna cleansed the wounds so as not to risk a transformation."

Michael chuckled. "Wendell, a werewolf." He shook his head. "Can't see it."

Obstein glanced at Wendell. "I am curious as to how it would change you with Nightmare already present," he mused, putting a finger to his chin in thought. Wendell's expression drastically changed to shock and Jacques made a choking sound.

Irving shook his head. "He has enough to worry about with the curse, Doctor. I would hate to see him burdened with anything else." In a low murmur, he added, "Witnessing the transformation was terrifying enough." There were dark circles under Irving's eyes and his usually smooth hair was untamed. Stubble had formed along his normally clean-shaven chin and jawline.

"You should sleep," Michael told his brother. "I am better now."

Obstein nodded his head in agreement. "Yes, as a doctor I must insist you rest, Irving." Wendell and Jacques nodded their heads in agreement.

"We will watch after him for you," Wendell told him.

Irving sighed, running a hand through his hair. "I guess you are all right. I shall head back to the inn and send Anna over."

Anna yelled with glee when she saw Michael awake and his wounds healed. She jumped up, clapping. "I was right! Immortality is the enemy of Death!" Michael smiled at her warmly, enduring her poking and prodding at the outline of the hoofprints.

"Yes, although the mortals are still very much in danger," Obstein stated. "We can hardly make everyone in the village immortal to avoid the curse's bite."

Anna paused to think. "Hmm, that is true."

"We have new information," Jacques said. Her interest piqued; she listened animatedly as he recounted the discussion with Nightmare that morning.

"And you have no memory of this?" Anna asked Wendell, who shook his head. "It must be that Nightmare can only speak through Wendell in human form, then."

"What do you think it meant?" Jacques asked.

"Hmmm," Anna paced a bit, thinking and twirling a loose strand of her hair. She turned back to him with a decided expression. "I have no idea!" she exclaimed.

# 21

# The Lively Fasching

## FIRST QUARTER MOON

**everal days passed as Anna,** Katharina, and Obstein tested their different theories on Wendell. The normally quiet village was filled with noise a week after the group tried to communicate with Nightmare. As Jacques walked down the path into town, a carriage filled with logs rolled past him, the horses snorting and flicking their tails. Jacques followed it, seeing the innkeeper with a wheelbarrow full of wood. Several people had come together near the center of the village, hammering and sawing away at the log pieces. He recognized the shape of tables and chairs in the later stages of the process. The baker's shop was producing more bread than usual; cakes, pies, and other desserts lined the shelves inside. Jacques passed by the butcher's shop and saw several pigs, sheep, and oxen in the livestock pen, as well as more meat hanging up to be cooked.

As he approached the inn, his throat dried up. Outside, Stuber was repairing part of the frontispiece. Several horses were hitched to the railing; most of which had packs tied to their saddles. A few men were tying their horses next to the others, and Jacques recognized their dirty and tattered uniforms as Catholic soldiers. He paused at the entrance, trying to swallow.

"About time you showed up," Stuber said from atop a ladder. "I could use an extra hand with preparations."

"What is the village preparing for?" Jacques asked.

Stuber stopped pounding at a nail and turned his attention to him. "The festival is in a few days. This time of year, we receive a lot of travelers that attend."

Jacques rolled his shoulders back, stretching out his injured arm. "How can I help?" he replied.

Stuber considered a response. "Well, we already have a few guests staying here. The tavern could use some tending to. Just keep bringing out the ale and they'll be happy."

Jacques dipped his head, going inside the inn. The tavern was on the first floor and full of people; but not just merchants and festive travelers. There were also more soldiers, perhaps a whole unit of men fresh from recent battle; some had bandages wrapped around their arms, legs, and heads. But their raucous laughter and loud conversations gave the impression they were in good spirits.

Jacques stilled in their presence, feeling sweat trickle down the back of his neck. He tried not to notice the symbols on their chests and patches on their shoulders denoting which side they were on. He walked through the tavern quickly, head down, and informed Stuber's wife he had come to help. She looked him up and down, then delegated him to the kitchen to clean dishes. It was hard work, but he preferred scrubbing plates to serving the men out there.

Jacques returned to Wendell's home when the sun began descending in the sky, sore and tired. He wondered how Wendell fared without him for the day, feeling a twinge of guilt for not coming back sooner. Opening the door, he felt a stark difference between the rush of people and sounds of clanging dishes compared to the quiet darkness of the still air inside. "Wendell?" he called softly. He heard a chair scrape against the floor and soon Wendell appeared in the hallway. Concern was replaced with a warm smile.

"I thought something had happened to you," Wendell said softly.

"Ah, my apologies," Jacques scratched the back of his neck. "I was asked to help with the festival preparations. I should have come back earlier."

Wendell stiffened. After a moment, he shook his head. "I am glad you are well enough to help, though I am sure Katharina wishes you not to overwork yourself."

Jacques ducked his head. "I shall try not to."

"Irving and the others returned to the inn not too long ago," Wendell said.

"Yes, I saw them on my way back and informed them about the upcoming festivities," Jacques replied. "How did it go today?"

Wendell scrunched up his nose. "Not as well as hoped, but I suppose it could have gone worse. Are you hungry? I prepared dinner."

Jacques was given a small plate at the tavern, but his stomach rumbled at the mention of more food. "I'm sorry I wasn't here to help," he said as he followed Wendell into the dining area. He thanked Wendell as a plate was placed in front of him. "You should see how lively the village has become." He said after a few bites.

Wendell's fork paused on its way to his mouth.

Jacques observed the other for a moment. "You should come with me tomorrow. It would do you well to get out of this house for a bit."

"I suppose." Wendell's lips pursed, forming a thin line.

"Is there something wrong?" Jacques asked, wondering if he had upset the other.

"I'm not allowed to participate in the festival," Wendell mumbled, eyes on his dish.

Jacques frowned. "Why not?" he asked, though the answer came to him before Wendell could reply. "Oh," he said in understanding.

"But you are welcome to go, I hear it is a wonderful time." Despite the resigned tone of his voice, there was a longing in Wendell's eyes.

"I could not forgive myself for going without you," Jacques told him. After a pause, he added, "What would your grandfather say?"

Wendell glanced at him. "He always said it was cruel to exclude me, but . . ." Jacques waited for him to finish silently. Wendell sighed and lowered his gaze back at his dinner. "But my parents always forbade it, and the villagers would scorn me for going. He took me, once, when I was a child. Even then, I could tell they were upset but could not understand why. They would not let me participate in activities with the other children, and eventually, he took me back home. My parents scolded him for taking me. I have never gone since."

A heavy sense of guilt bore down on Jacques for helping with something Wendell was forbidden to attend. "I won't go either, then." He stabbed into a piece of meat and chewed aggressively. He felt Wendell's eyes on him and saw a small smile form out of the corner of his eye.

## WAXING GIBBOUS MOON

On the day of the *fasching*, Jacques heard carts and the stamping of hooves passing. Music played in the distance, along with laughter and loud conversation. He walked out onto the porch, where the smell of sweets and fresh meats wafted through the air. Jacques glanced back to Wendell standing in the doorway, watching people pour into the village.

Irving and Luis emerged from the crowd passing by the house and came up the steps. Luis had a scowl on his face and darkness beneath his eyes.

"All this ruckus for such a small place," he grumbled.

Irving was smiling, ever the opposite of his companion. "Anna got distracted at all the merchant's tents on the way over. I'm quite interested, myself."

"Where is Michael?" Wendell asked with a concerned face.

"He's still at the apothecary. Crowds make him nervous," Irving replied.

Wendell nodded, rubbing his arms. "I can understand why."

"Maybe we can check it out later, once the visitors have settled," Irving said, glancing to Luis.

Luis snorted. "You can go by yourself. Anna is probably harassing a merchant for some strange ingredients again."

"I thought you loved crowds?" Irving teased him.

"Only for easy pickpocketing."

Wendell was silent as they talked, Jacques frowning with his arms crossed. Irving raised an eyebrow. "Is something wrong?" he asked.

"They won't let Wendell participate because of the curse, so we don't plan on going," Jacques replied.

"But *you* should go," Wendell added with a reassuring smile. "I'm sure they would love for you to participate."

Irving and Luis glanced at each other in determination before turning their attention back to Jacques and Wendell.

The two found themselves going into town despite their protests. Sandwiched between Irving and Luis, they had no choice but to follow the crowd. While still cold, the air was crisp and refreshing as they made their way down the dirt path. The sun peeked out amongst the clouds, warm against their skin. As they neared the town square, Jacques could almost taste the spice of cider on his tongue, warm and comforting. Several tents were set up where merchants and villagers alike sold wares and made food for participants. A few children were playing in the streets while their parents gathered around to talk and laugh. His eyes kept falling on military uniforms, quickly averting his gaze whenever a soldier turned his way.

"I fear this will not go well," Wendell whispered in a strained voice.

"We will ensure no harm comes to you," Irving told him. "It is simply ridiculous that they try to deprive you of simple worldly pleasures. I cannot believe you've never once been able to play as a child." His tone was stern and expression fierce, conveying his displeasure at what Wendell told them moments before.

Jacques noticed Luis swiftly placing his hand back inside his pants pocket with a slight smirk on his face. The hunter's eyes met his and Jacques chuckled.

"Luis," Irving hissed, swatting at his arm.

Luis shrugged. "They deserve it."

"Hey!" a shout alerted the group. Jacques tensed as he searched for the source of the voice.

"What are you doing here?" Bäcker asked from his table, bristling. The locals turned toward them and began to whisper amongst themselves, pointing at Wendell and frowning. Wendell halted; shoulders hunching, legs bracing, and arms stiffening at his side as he felt the weight of their glares hard on his back. Jacques took Wendell's hand.

"He has every right to enjoy the festival as you do," Jacques told the baker.

"No. He should not be here," the man said, shaking his head vigorously.

"Why cause a fuss with visitors around and ruin the merriment of the day?" Irving asked the baker, quirking an eyebrow up and stepping forward.

Bäcker spluttered, grasping a rolling pin tightly until his hand turned red. "The cursed one is forbidden to partake in this festival! It has always been this way," he seethed.

Irving surveyed the crowds of people and then Bäcker. "If you are referring to Wendell, it is my professional opinion as an Inquisitor that he is harmless in his current state, and therefore should be allowed to enjoy the festival just like you and I."

Locals and visitors alike began to take an interest in the confrontation between the group and the baker, enough to draw attention from the priest.

"Ah, welcome guests!" Father Heinrich exclaimed as he moved through the crowd in full ceremonial robes. His expression darkened upon seeing Wendell but was otherwise pleasant. "I am so pleased to see you enjoying the festivities that our village has worked so hard to put on."

"There seems to be an issue concerning Wendell's presence here," Irving stated, staring straight into the clergyman's eyes. "Would you care to help us put this matter aside for good and all?" His voice was calm and charming, but ferocity was still present in his eyes.

Father Heinrich observed Bäcker, who did not appear to back down, and to the onlookers; some faces showing curiosity and concern, while others showing disdain. "Let us discuss this elsewhere, so as not to disrupt—"

"No, here is fine. If this is a village matter, I would prefer the villagers to weigh in on it," Irving challenged. Wendell was uncomfortable, leaning closer to Jacques and squeezing his hand tightly. Luis was right beside them, glaring at the priest.

With visible effort, Father Heinrich exhaled a breath and schooled his expression. "Very well, I understand." He turned to the gathered locals, using a charming disposition to bestow calmness. "Is anyone opposed to the inclusion of our . . . special guest in today's activities?"

Merchants and travelers carried on as if witnessing one of the village's traditions, eyes filled with wonder as they took in the "special guest" Father Heinrich was referring to. Clearly, those in the know were torn between outright opposition and quiet agreement. Shifting and murmuring occurred within those gathered.

"This is absurd," the baker spat. He opened his mouth to continue but paused as the eyes of strangers set upon him.

Irving gave him an expectant look, folding his arms over his chest. "What is absurd about including this particular young man?"

"You know exactly why—"

"Could you then explain it to those who are not aware?" Irving interrupted, gesturing to the curious spectators.

"There is no need," Father Heinrich said quickly. He locked eyes with Bäcker. "Some traditions become unnecessary over time and under certain circumstances. I believe today is as good a day as any to make such a change."

Bäcker's jaw clenched, but he did not dispute the priest's words. "Of course, Father."

Father Heinrich nodded. "It is settled, then! Please, enjoy the festival as much as you like," he proclaimed. Some newcomers cheered at his words, and the crowd dispersed.

Irving's grin resembled a man who had won a war. As they pressed on, Luis took a cookie from the table and bit into it. Bäcker scowled at him.

With the issue resolved, the villagers did not try to stop the group as they continued through the festival. Wendell and Jacques were still walking hand-in-hand. Jacques feared that letting go would unleash their vitriol; and Wendell's hand was warm in his.

"That was well done," Obstein said to Irving as he came out of the mass of people.

Irving's grin widened. "Hopefully that will deter them from any further provocations against Wendell."

Obstein nodded his head in agreement. "Indeed. I'm sure Albrecht would be proud."

Jacques glanced to see Wendell's reaction to the doctor's words. His large eyes were bright with moisture. Jacques gave his hand a light squeeze. Wendell turned to him with the biggest smile he had ever seen on the other. Tears of happiness glistened in the light of the sun. Jacques beamed back at him.

# 22

# The Stirring Schuhplattler

**A**nna bounded up to them shortly after the incident with the baker, her arms full of various items. She had an excited gleam in her eyes.

"Look what I found!" She shoved the contents in front of Irving and Luis. They picked up a bottle and bag of herbs, examining them. "I was fortunate to find a merchant selling these kinds of items here; he came from a long way off. I want to see if I can use these for more experiments!" Her expression took on a maniacal tone that the others seemed used to.

"I'd like to explore around as well," Irving said. He turned to Wendell and Jacques. "You should be free of any trouble now, so enjoy the activities."

"Are you sure?" Wendell asked nervously, glancing around at all the people gathered. He gripped Jacques' hand tighter.

Luis tipped his head. "We'll keep an eye on you."

Anna was already tugging Irving toward a stall with wares. Luis caught up before they got lost amongst the festivities.

"Well, what would you like to do first?" Jacques asked.

Wendell turned around. It was the first time he had seen so many people in the village, let alone all the decorations and activities laid out. He homed in on something beyond the throng. "Do you hear that?"

Jacques listened closely but could barely pick up the music in between loud conversations. He followed Wendell, who led them toward the noise.

In the center of the town square, a group of young men wearing matching sets of lederhosen with white shirts and wooden shoes were dancing, accompanied by a band of musicians. They clapped as they walked around in a circle, then stopped to lift one knee, slapping their thighs in a rhythmic fashion. Then they started hopping around, slapping their knees and the soles of their shoes to a happy beat.

"What is that?" Jacques asked.

"The *Schuhplattler*, I believe," Wendell replied. He dipped his head, shyly tucking some hair behind his ear. "Well, at least it appears to be from the books I read. I have yet to see a live performance."

"Ah," Jacques replied, grinning. "The people of my town do something similar."

They watched the dancers, both for the first time, in awe. Jacques felt something strong bubbling up inside of his chest, rising with each jump and slap. He did not realize it was excitement until he let go of Wendell's hand to applaud and yell with the rest of the audience at the end of the performance.

"I wish to learn," Wendell said in a rush as the praise died down around them. His smile faltered as some of the locals tittered at him, shaking their heads as they moved away from the pair.

Jacques turned to him, smile still wide and bright. "We should both learn!" Before Wendell could object, Jacques was pulling him toward the group of young dancers. "Excuse me, could you teach us how to do that dance?"

The dancers eyed Wendell warily. "Not him," one said.

Jacques' nostrils flared and he let out a loud sigh, his breath misty in the air. He was about to speak when Wendell waved him off. "It is fine, I shall be happy just to watch."

"You have every right to learn as I do," Jacques told him.

"The cursed one is forbidden from participating," one of the young dancers stated, as if reciting from a book.

Jacques gritted his teeth. "Father Heinrich declared that Wendell may join the festival, which includes any activities therein."

The dancers muttered to themselves, casting confused glances at one another and gesturing toward Wendell.

Wendell took both of Jacques' hands into his own. "I do not wish for any more confrontations. Please, learn for me." He leaned closer. "You can teach me later," he whispered.

Jacques opened his mouth, words at the tip of his tongue, ready to tell Wendell anything he needed. Instead, he dipped his head.

Wendell squeezed Jacques' hand and then let go. Jacques watched as he found a spot to sit down, knees curling up to his chest and arms wrapping around them, closing himself off again.

The dancers reluctantly took Jacques into their circle and started teaching him the rhythm of the dance. Jacques caught Wendell watching as he practiced the basic movement, balancing on one leg and hopping around with the other dancers. The young men then demonstrated by slapping their thighs and shoes slowly. Jacques lifted his leg, swaying a bit until he gained balance, and then slapped his thigh where they showed him.

"It has to be harder—louder," a dancer said. "It hurts, but you get used to it."

Jacques nodded and repeated the action, the sound resounding around the area. When he tried it with his wounded arm, he winced after only a light hit. The dancers noticed the stitches on his arm, and some glanced toward Wendell. Jacques laughed it off and insisted on trying it again with his good arm.

When it was time for the dancers to perform again, Jacques sat down next to Wendell. He was breathless, palms red and blistering. He rolled up his pants to reveal red spots on his thighs, some already beginning to bruise. "It's painful, but fun."

Wendell smiled back at him. "I am glad they agreed to teach you."

"I just wish you could join as well," Jacques said, smile fading.

Wendell laughed. "Not if it hurts that much."

Jacques smiled and laughed back. "They said if I learn it fast enough, I can perform with them on the last day of the festival."

"Perform? Are you well enough to do that?"

Jacques nodded his head. "But I told them only if you're my partner." He gazed into Wendell's eyes.

Wendell took in a breath. "Do you think they will let me?" he asked quietly. He couldn't tear away from Jacques' stare.

Jacques glanced away, rubbing the back of his head. "I'm still convincing them. Anyway, I'm starved. Let us eat!"

A whole pig was being roasted on a spit over an open fire, with freshly grown vegetables and fruits laid out on tables nearby. Sausage links and other meats were served on platters. Several townspeople were serving out the feast. Wendell and Jacques got in line with plates. There were many confused or wary glances at Wendell's involvement, but his plate was eventually loaded up with food and they headed over to a table.

"We saw you dancing," Irving announced as he joined them with a plate of his own. He gave Jacques a curious smile, his eyes glinting with a certain mischievousness.

Jacques replied excitedly, "They're teaching me their dance, but it's a bit hard."

"Why didn't you join in?" Luis asked Wendell as he stole a piece of meat from Irving's plate.

"They . . . did not want me to," Wendell replied, pushing his vegetables around. "But Jacques is magnificent at it!" he added quickly, smiling at the other.

Irving sighed. "Then we must try harder to get the locals to accept you."

"I told them I would perform with them on the final day if they allowed Wendell to join," Jacques stated.

"You don't have to do this for me, really," Wendell said, squirming in his seat. "I cause enough trouble."

Luis snorted. "Not enough, in my opinion," he said, spearing another piece of Irving's food with his fork.

Irving nudged Luis with his elbow. "Hey, you have your own plate," he said, although his tone did not sound serious.

"I like yours better," Luis replied, biting down on the sausage. The two stared at each other for a moment, as if no one else was around.

Wendell glanced away at his own dish. Jacques' gaze traveled across the other tables, catching a few locals and travelers watching Luis and Irving—at the way they were gazing at each other, how close they were sitting next to each other. Jacques observed how differently they acted toward each other than the others and had an idea as to why the festival goers were tittering and shaking their heads. His skin prickled.

## WAXING GIBBOUS MOON

"Well, I suppose if Father Heinrich gave his blessing," one of the dancers said the next day, barely acknowledging Wendell, "you are welcome to join us."

Wendell could not stop a smile from spreading across his face as a rare moment of hope overcame him. He turned to Jacques, who grinned back at him.

"It goes like this, yes?" Jacques demonstrated a part of the dance by lifting his leg and slapping his thighs.

"Yes, good," one of the other dancers said.

Jacques gestured to Wendell. "Now you try!"

Hesitating, Wendell lifted his leg, and then lightly tapped it in the same manner. He eyed Jacques for reassurance.

"A bit harder," Jacques coaxed him. Wendell nodded and tried again, wincing at first as he hit himself harder. "Yes, you've got it! Now try faster."

They kept practicing, taking turns learning the moves from the seasoned dancers who at first hesitated to engage with Wendell. But after a light conversation, they became enamored with the brightness of his smile and relaxed more around him. When the older men performed, they watched and discussed the movements amongst themselves.

"Maybe if the whole village sees you participating, they will be more understanding," Jacques said.

"I don't know . . ." Wendell tucked some of his hair behind his ear. Despite the cold weather, he felt warm from all the movement. "Not much has changed here over the years. It may take them a lot longer to truly feel comfortable around someone like me."

"They just have to get to know you, like I did, and the Inquisitors have," Jacques told him. "Your grandfather told me that you were the gentlest person to come under this curse. He wanted me to stay with you; not just to look after you, but to get to know you better. He was convinced that your soft nature was enough to melt the snow in winter." Jacques chuckled. He avoided Wendell's gaze, dismissing the heat in his cheeks as effort from the dance.

Wendell's fingers wound their way through his. "Thank you," he whispered.

## WAXING GIBBOUS MOON

On the last day of the festival, Wendell rubbed his hands together, fidgeting out of nervousness. He wore the traditional lederhosen—a bit too tight for him. He remembered when it was too big, and the brief time when it had fit just right.

The music started and the group of dancers began to move. One after the other, they slapped the flat part of one hand against a closed fist as they marched onto the stage, forming a circle. Then they stopped, lifting one leg up and hopping up and down as they raised their arms overhead before conducting elaborate clapping maneuvers. The sharp sounds pierced the air as they slapped their legs, the soles of their shoes, and their hands together while jumping from one foot to the other. The slaps were in time with the music, punctuating each note. Wendell kept his eyes on Jacques, heart racing while his breath came out sharp and fast. He attempted to focus solely on the dance, trying to remember the patterns and steps. He refused to see the faces staring at him but could sense the shock, disappointment, and fury wafting off the locals. The guests were smiling, clapping along to the music, but some of the villagers did not appear to be amused.

Wendell caught sight of Irving, Luis, Anna, and even Michael in the crowd. Irving and Anna were clapping joyously along with the music, smiling at him. Michael had a pleasant expression, and even Luis seemed to be enjoying the entertainment. Wendell let out a breath, releasing some of the tension in his limbs. He danced more freely, allowing himself to smile and sing with the other dancers more loudly.

It was almost over too soon, and at the end, each dancer took a girl waiting in front of the crowd and spun her around so her dirndl twirled. Jacques reached out to Wendell, who hesitated until he saw Jacques' reassuring smile. Wendell took his hand and was spun.

At the end of the dance, Jacques kept hold of Wendell's hand and bowed with the other dancers. Wendell tentatively bowed back. Low murmurs and dark eyes were all around them.

"He should not have been allowed to dance," a villager muttered.

"How disgraceful," another added viciously.

Wendell was the only one who could hear them from where the dancers were on stage. His eyes darted around to the speakers, chest heaving. His skin was tingling and sweat beaded upon his brow. It was just like when he was a child, holding tightly onto his grandfather's leather pants as people pointed angrily at him and spat in his face.

Jacques placed his hands gently on either side of his head. "Hey, keep your eyes on me. Ignore them. I won't let them hurt you." Wendell stared into Jacques' eyes, letting the malevolence around them fade until there was nothing but the two of them.

"That was wonderful!" Irving said gleefully, clapping. The crowd dispersed, only a few lingering behind to glare at the pair.

Anna hugged Wendell tightly. "You did so well! I'm proud of the progress you've made in such a short time!"

Wendell was not sure how to respond but hugged her back. "Thank you."

"Is he not a natural?" Jacques boasted. "I barely had to help him!"

"Good dance," one of the lederhosen-clad young men said, nodding toward Wendell. He shook Jacques' hand. "You should both join us next time."

"No," an older dancer growled. He spat on the ground in front of Wendell. Other men glared at Wendell with disdain. "You have defiled our traditions. Stay home if you have any sense of decency."

"There is no need to be vile," Irving hissed, stepping toward the man.

"You lot stay out of this," the man replied, scowling at Irving. His eyes narrowed.

Luis and Michael stepped up on either side of Irving, fists clenched. Wendell sensed the anger and animosity in the air. His body tensed with the expectancy of a fight. Anna put a hand on his shoulder, an unreadable expression on her face.

"Do you take issue with our presence here?" Irving

asked challengingly.

"I take issue with the way you act with *him*," the man pointed to Luis. "Your kind belongs in hell."

Irving said nothing, his eyes widening. Luis made to move but Michael held him back. Jacques recoiled at the man's words as if struck with the knowledge of their relationship. He checked on Wendell, who had a sad expression.

The older dancer continued. "We thought you'd come to help us end this curse, but you've only made it worse by flaunting your sinful behavior and influencing the cursed one. Leave now or be thrown out."

Irving's eyes took on a sharp gleam, as if able to cut the man down like a knife. "Is that a threat?" he asked in a low, slow voice. It gave Wendell the sense of a predator about to strike at its prey.

The older man lifted his chin in a daring way. "If you want to settle it like men, I'll let you have the first swing."

Michael let go of Luis to grab hold of Irving's arm as it coiled back. "Brother," he said. It was all he needed to say.

Irving took a deep breath, closing his eyes for a moment as he regained his composure. He walked away with an edge in his step, parting the crowd with his intimidating aura. Michael and Anna turned after him, but Luis remained rooted to his spot.

Until the moment he launched forward, fist colliding with the other man's gut. The dancer doubled over. Another man pounced on Luis, who kicked at his legs. One grabbed hold of Luis' arm, holding him while the first man lifted his fist.

Jacques took a step forward, but Irving rushed past him and tackled the dancer to the ground, grappling with him. Shouts arose as the brawl continued. Anna whacked one of the people fighting Luis, but Michael pulled her back.

"Get them to safety," he growled out. Wendell could hear a tonal shift in his vocal cords and knew he was close to transforming.

Anna huffed, grabbing Wendell and Jacques, who protested.

"We have to help them!" Jacques pulled back from her grip, turning toward the fight.

"They can handle it," Anna told him. She quickly dragged them to a less populated area as more people joined the fighting; some trying to stop it, others encouraging it. The cacophony of shouts and flesh hitting flesh was all Wendell could hear.

# 23

# The Misguided Mob

In the aftermath, Irving's nose was broken while Luis had a black eye and swollen cheek. Their knuckles were bruised and bloody and their clothes were covered in dirt. Michael was unharmed yet unhappy. They were all gathered in Wendell's home with the doors locked. Most of the festival's visitors had packed up and left after witnessing the fight, distressed over the oddities and animosity of the village or afraid for their own lives, some refusing to come back. Doubtless the villagers were even angrier after losing the rare bit of commerce they had relied on.

"Nice job, boys," Anna said in a sarcastic manner.

Luis scowled; arms folded. "I couldn't let them get away with it," he said through gritted teeth.

"So, you start a fight with the entire community when they already bode us ill will?" she replied sternly.

Irving frowned at her, holding a washcloth over his nose. "They provoked us," he said, voice muffled and distorted.

"Should not have fought," Michael grumbled. His voice was more strained than normal, veins popping out of his arms.

Irving removed the bloody cloth and breathed in. "They were going to kill Luis," he said softly.

"I would have taken a few of them down with me," Luis said beside him.

Irving turned to him, brushing his thumb across the untouched cheek. "Please don't be reckless like that again, love."

Luis uncrossed his arms and leaned closer, kissing Irving on the lips chastely. "Sorry," he murmured against the other's lips.

Loud voices shattered the night, darkness scattered by the light of torches in the crisp air. It turned charged, electric, as a mob approached Wendell's home. He spotted them through the window. Jacques was beside him, hand pressing against the wall near the window as he glared out at the residents who were shouting.

"This can go on no longer!"

"We can't let that thing exist!"

"Execute the cursed one!"

"The Inquisitors have fallen in with the devil!"

"Kill them all!"

Wendell's face went pale, his body cold. They were calling for all their deaths—not just his own.

"They don't seem to learn, do they?" Luis muttered, getting up to survey the group outside.

Irving started moving quickly behind them, gathering their belongings. Michael hastily grabbed food and blankets throughout the house. Anna dumped her tools and supplies inside of her bag.

Jacques glanced between them. "What are you doing?"

"We have to leave," Irving replied as he packed. "You're no longer safe in this village, Wendell. None of us are. We have effectively outstayed our welcome."

Wendell turned to him with a woeful expression. "I was never safe."

Irving paused, regarding the young man's face with sharp sorrow.

Then he glanced at his comrades. "Luis, Michael, create a diversion."

"Already on it," Luis said as he picked up a broom and broke it in half across his leg. Wendell was mildly concerned about his things being broken, but Jacques was tugging on his arm toward Irving and Anna while Luis and Michael stood in front of the door, holding makeshift weapons.

"Anything you wish to bring with you? Now is the time to get it." Irving asked. "It is unlikely you will ever return here."

Wendell thought about what he could take with him, but every item he saw brought back painful memories. With a sharp intake of breath, he rushed to his room where the last carving his grandfather had done, a buck with many branching antlers, sat on a table near his bed and clutched it to his chest. He gathered some blankets, extra clothes, and soap, then tore the lunar calendar off the wall, wrapping them up in one of the blankets.

"Is that all?" Jacques asked him, stuffing his grungy backpack with more supplies.

"There is nothing left here for me," Wendell replied solemnly. Everything else had already been taken from him.

"Let's move; they'll distract the villagers and meet up with us later," Irving said as he turned down the hallway. Anna ushered Wendell and Jacques ahead of her.

There was a thud as the door swung open and shouts grew louder as the mob collided with the two at the front of the old wooden house. Jacques placed a steady hand on Wendell's shoulder. Irving paused at the back door, putting his ear to the wood. Wendell heard the scuffle in the other room; curses being yelled, grunts of pain, furniture being shoved.

And then footsteps pounded through the house to match the frantic beating of Wendell's heart. He whirled around to the light of flames coming closer to the hall; already feeling the heat of the fire and smelling the smoke that came with it, his eyes burning.

"Run!" Irving yelled, and they took off.

Bursting through the back door, Wendell faced ahead, hearing his breathing loud in his ears as his legs moved across the ground. He glanced behind him when he registered that only Jacques was running with him. Irving and Anna were standing at the back door, preparing to fight off the people who got past Luis and Michael.

"Don't look back, just keep going!" Jacques shouted. Wendell noticed he was slowing down and hurried to catch up. Out of the corner of his eye, he saw flickering lights rounding the corner of the house, coming toward them at an angle on either side. Jacques was swearing in his native tongue as they swerved away from the oncoming townspeople. Behind them, flames were reaching toward the sky and licking at their heels as the house burned to the ground. Wendell saw Irving punch one of the older men from before with his bare hands, while Anna threw vials of liquid from her bag at the ones coming after him. Some of them screamed and threw up their hands to avoid the fluids, their skin hissing and charring at whatever poison was inside, before turning back on her.

"To the woods!" Jacques pulled on Wendell's arm, dragging him into the woods directly behind the house. The villagers were closing in on them from both sides. They were not fast enough.

Wendell felt hands on him, grabbing him, pulling him away from Jacques. He cried out, reaching. Jacques turned and yelled his name, unable to pursue as he too was dragged back. Fleischer had him by the arms, and Wendell could see the strain on his injured shoulder weaken him.

A sack was placed over his head and suddenly all was darkness. His senses were already magnified, but blind they only increased—the feeling of people's hands on him, the twigs and loose ground beneath his bare feet, his breath coming out ragged, shouts and cries, the heat from the fire held so close to him. He flinched away, trying to struggle, but was soon bound by thick, scratchy rope. They forced him to run at a steady pace, keeping their hands on his arms, pulling him up when he tripped over branches or dug in his heels.

He didn't know where he was being taken until the sack was removed from his head. They were deep within the forest, where the sounds of the town were muffled. Wendell could still hear the crackling of the fire, though. He swept his eyes around the small clearing. Jacques was there too, gagged, but staring at him. Wendell remembered what Jacques had said after they danced the *Schuhplattler* and people began murmuring their dissent. *"Keep your eyes on me. Ignore them. I won't let them hurt you."*

That same intensity was in his eyes now as they were both brought to their knees. Fleischer pulled out one of his knives made for gutting pigs and placed it under Jacques' throat. The curve of a blade made for harvesting crops was placed at Wendell's own neck. But he didn't acknowledge the scythe or the people he had grown up around. He only focused on Jacques, his messy hair, his deep blue eyes, and his dirty torn tunic, once freshly white.

He took one deep, final breath and closed his eyes, awaiting the end. In the silence of the moment, however, he heard something else within the woods. Feet were running toward them, one set heavy with the bulk of a large man, the other lighter and swifter. Wendell's eyes snapped open as Michael burst through one side of the clearing without stopping, plowing into Fleischer and taking him down to the ground. Jacques surged to his feet, hands still tied behind his back, to kick out his legs and force the hold on him to break. The scythe, which had been lifted to strike, was knocked aside by Luis who darted in while the others focused on Michael and Fleischer wrestling on the ground. With a small knife, Luis lunged at the people closest to Wendell.

Danger and fear coalesced until Wendell started to feel it happening, more aware than ever before of his oncoming transition. He saw a bright moon, almost full—not the one he was used to seeing when such a feeling overcame him. But his head pounded and his vision swarmed as the urge to fight back overcame him. He was not scared. An emotion he rarely gave yield to began bubbling up within the depths of his chest: red hot and seething.

"Fight it!" Jacques shouted as he freed himself of the gag. He ran toward Wendell as points pushed through his blond hair and his feet became hooved. Fur began covering his arms, which elongated and ended in long, hooked claws.

The villagers started backing away—even Luis took a few steps back—as Nightmare fully emerged. But Wendell had not lost control. He took a step forward, feeling himself move, controlling his own actions. And yet he could not stop the rage from overwhelming him— the feeling turned instinctual as the being within began guiding his actions instead of commanding them.

"Wendell," Jacques' eyes were full of fear, his hand stretched out as if to stop him.

"Now! Kill it now!" Fleischer shouted from the ground where Michael held him.

A rock was thrown at Nightmare, the solid surface hitting its side and shattering into smaller pieces before bouncing back to the ground. It turned toward the one who threw the rock.

"No! Nightmare, don't!" Jacques called before Nightmare let out a piercing roar and charged forward, antlers pointed. The offender did not have time to get out of the way and was skewered on the sharp ends, lifted high in the air, and thrown roughly into a tree on the other side of the clearing. The man thudded to the ground, dead.

Nightmare heard the scythe swinging in the air and moved, using one massive back hoof to kick the wielder, who went down.

"It's not enough, we need more people," Fleischer gasped out.

Nightmare began stalking toward him. Michael moved away from the butcher, but Jacques got in between them.

"Think about what you're doing, Wendell. It's not worth it. You're letting Nightmare control you. Fight it!"

*I am the one in control,* Wendell thought, his own voice mixing with the timbre of the creature inside his mind. The two worked as one as Nightmare took another step forward. Jacques was still standing in front of it, arms out, closer than anyone else dared to get.

Nightmare and Wendell were aware of the hunters watching and the mob encircling around. Fear and anger wafted up from the humans, while death and decay spread all around as the grass turned gray and disintegrated under the death stag's hooves. Their nostrils flared and hot air blew out of them, lifting a few hairs from Jacques' head.

Jacques refused to move an inch. "You'll have to kill me first. I won't let you do this to yourself," Jacques said. His eyes were locked onto the monster's, alight with determination. And fear. "Wendy, *please.*"

A sharp pain made Nightmare cry out, whirling around to the source. The butcher was holding knives in his shaking hand, ready to throw more. Nightmare reared up with a roar, striking the ground so heavily that it caused a small fissure that raced toward Fleischer. The man fell back as if struck directly, groaning and writhing on the ground.

Someone else yelled, running at the creature with a scythe in hand. They swung, but the monster's antlers caught the blade and yanked it from the man's hands. It landed with a thump several feet away. A rope was slung around the antlers and a few men pulled, forcing Nightmare's head to turn and let out a guttural sound.

"Wait!" Jacques yelled, running forward to block a blow to the creature's throat.

"Why are you helping it?" Bäcker shouted, tugging on the rope.

"Because I love him!" Jacques shouted back. "And I made a promise to protect him from *you!*"

Wendell understood the words through the cacophony of chaos within Nightmare's head and faltered. A wellspring of hope filled his heart at the confession, and they renewed their efforts to fight off the mob attempting to slay the beast. As they wrestled with the rope tangled within their antlers, they saw Irving and Michael grappling with the men holding on to the other end. They swung their head around, almost nicking Jacques who was struggling to remove the rope from Nightmare's points. But the rope was tangled up too much. Nightmare stamped its hooves in frustration. They felt something grab onto their flank and almost reared to throw it off until they noticed Jacques had climbed onto their back and toward their head.

"Quit moving," Jacques hissed into their ear. Nightmare snorted but paused as Jacques reached out with quivering arms and sweaty palms to unloop the rope from the juncture it got caught in. Once free, Nightmare shook its head, lifting it high. They felt Jacques hold on tightly to their rough, matted fur and bone as they charged forward.

Irving and Michael dove out of the way. Bäcker stared in shock before the beast's points went through him, nailing him to a tree.

"Please, Wendy, *stop*," Jacques whispered in a desperate tone. Wet droplets soaked into Nightmare's fur. They released the baker, who slid down to the ground with a slump, and took in the ones who remained in the clearing.

Luis had one of the remaining villagers restrained, watching Nightmare with sharp eyes. Irving's hand reached for his gun as the beast turned toward him. Michael gave out a low warning growl.

Anna stood still, peering into Nightmare's eyes as if she could find Wendell through them. She had a few bottles clenched in her hand, but the other was raised and steady. "Peace, Wendell," she said in a calm tone.

Nightmare turned its head toward her, saliva dripping from its maw.

"Please," Jacques pleaded.

Anna was chanting low, her eyes closed and palm out. Wendell could not understand what she was saying, but it was having an effect on Nightmare. The creature's rage began to dim and they stilled, listening to her spell. The animosity swarming the air dissipated into serenity. The smell of fear on Jacques evaporated, replaced with calm. His fingers relaxed their grip on Nightmare's fur, and they felt him slide down their back. He went over to where Anna was standing, no longer tense or apprehensive. Seeing the man who loved him safe and no longer afraid erased all thoughts of destruction from Wendell's mind, and he could feel Nightmare fading.

Wendell blinked his large eyes and felt the antlers and bony fur receding painlessly until he found himself on his hands and knees in front of them, clothes hanging torn from his body. He leaned forward until his forehead touched the ground and cried.

Jacques rushed forward as he saw Wendell return, holding him. "Everything is all right now, you're fine, I'm fine. We are all safe now, Wendy."

Irving appeared from behind the trees, out of breath and covered in soot. Anna let out a deep breath, opening her eyes. Luis knelt down to wipe the blood off of his knife on the dead grass before sheathing it and standing.

"This is all the proof we need," he said, turning to Irving.

"Yes," Irving replied, walking forward with a grim expression.

"Don't touch him!" Jacques yelled, once again putting himself between Wendell and danger. "I won't let you hurt him!" He held onto Wendell tightly, eyes wild as they darted from one to the other.

"Relax," Irving said, kneeling down next to Wendell. "We shall not harm him." He tentatively placed a hand on Wendell's shuddering back.

Michael came around to help Wendell up. "You did it."

Wendell's eyes roamed blearily, face wet and head aching. "Did what?" he rasped out.

"You learned how to control Nightmare," Anna whispered gently, running her fingers through Wendell's sweaty, disheveled hair.

"And *you* stopped him from doing more harm," Luis stated, gesturing to Jacques.

They were all focused on Jacques as if they'd found the answer. Jacques just stared back at them, still clutching Wendell's shivering, sobbing form.

"You realize what this means, don't you?" Irving said softly with a steady hand still comforting Wendell. When Jacques just blinked at him, mouth open, he continued. "You must stay with him always, Jacques. He needs you."

# 24

# The Next Journey

## WAXING GIBBOUS MOON

**A**s the light of early dawn filtered through the darkness of the sky, they all left the village on horseback. The townspeople stood just on the edge of the forest, watching them. Irving and Luis managed to secure their horses and saddle them, all under the cold gazes of the villagers, who did nothing to stop them from leaving.

"They were not trying to kill you," Irving explained. "They were trying to drive you out, or make make Nightmare appear so they could attack it since they knew destroying the vessel did no good."

"They assumed that killing the beast in its true form would relieve them of the curse," Anna added. "Though it would probably just continue in its cycle of rebirth in another. You would have been the only one to die."

Luis snorted. "They're still ignorant to think it would work." He sat behind Irving on one of the horses they rode into the village on.

"Send the curse somewhere else, so they wouldn't have to deal with it anymore," Jacques muttered, disdain dripping from his voice.

"I don't mind," Wendell said serenely. He was calmer now with the awareness that he had gained a sense of control—and camaraderie—with Nightmare. The townspeople had left them alone to part rather peacefully, his home nothing but smoldering ash behind them. "I always wanted to travel."

Jacques glanced back at him; Wendell's arms were wrapped around his waist. "I guess it worked out for us after all." His smile was wide and bright.

Wendell's cheeks flushed pink, and he tucked some hair behind his ear.

"Where would you like to go first?" Irving asked. They all looked to Wendell, waiting.

The flames from the mob still felt so close to Wendell, even though they had traveled some distance away. The angry faces of people he had known his whole life filled his dreams. Yet the further they got from his home, the more weight was lifted from his shoulders. Finally free from the burden of being a scapegoat for the village's sins, Wendell could finally just be himself. It was exhilarating and terrifying. He knew where they needed to go next. "I think we should continue my grandfather's search for answers," Wendell replied. "I want to go to Jacques' village."

The group agreed, and with the right starting direction from Jacques (as far as he could tell), they headed southwest through the forest, where the vegetation was gray and no birds sang to guide their journey.

## FULL MOON

They stuck mostly to the gravel roads and grassy trails carved out by previous travelers but stopped in a small town for fresh food and more comfortable sleeping arrangements on the second day out. It was the night of a full moon, so Michael secluded himself in one of the rooms as soon as they arrived.

"Ahhh," Anna stretched her arms above her head as she propped her feet up on the table. "All this travel is starting to get to me."

Irving glared at her feet, frowning. She noticed his staring, as well as the disgusted murmurs from the other tavern patrons, and quickly brought them back to the ground with a sheepish expression.

"It's only been a few days," Luis scoffed.

"Yes, but I was just getting used to staying at Wendell's village," she replied.

Jacques glanced at Wendell. "How are you feeling?"

Wendell let out a slow breath. He had never traveled this long or been on a horse for so many hours at a time. "Sore," he admitted. With a smile, he added, "But I'm glad to go on this journey with you."

Jacques smiled back at him. Wendell felt his face grow warm—his entire *body* grow warm—at the way Jacques looked at him. It was a pleasant feeling, if unfamiliar.

"Here you go," their server said as she put down plates of hot fresh food: oxtail soup, fresh cherries, and plums with bread. She also set down cups of the local beer, the golden liquid sloshing. "My name is Mina, please let me know if there is anything else you need." She gave a small curtsy in greeting.

"Thank you," Irving said as the others dug into the food.

"Mina!" someone called into the tavern and their server searched for the speaker, her long dark hair swishing around her. A boy was waving her over with enthusiasm. She gave a soft smile and made a gesture back.

"Excuse me," Mina dipped her head and left their table to greet the boy.

"So young," Anna said around her mouthful of food. "They look to be about your age," she gestured to Wendell and Jacques.

Wendell saw Mina and the young man talking with each other in a corner of the tavern, standing close. By the expression on their faces, it was clear they were smitten with each other. Wendell cleared his throat and went back to his food, feeling as if he were witnessing a private moment.

They were undisturbed for the rest of their meal. An older woman came to pick up the empty plates. Shaking her head at the young couple, who were still shyly talking in a corner of the tavern, she let out a sigh. "Young ones in love, they are too distracted to do their work."

"It's romantic," Anna said, smiling.

"Not when they're always running off together and shirking their duties," the older woman mumbled as she left.

After Anna's third beer, Irving said, "We should get some rest." She had become loud and raunchy, slapping the table and talking quickly of her experiments, to the confusion of the tavern patrons.

Upon leaving the establishment, Anna slightly swerving as they ambled down the street, Wendell spotted Mina and the young boy in the alleyway beside the tavern, tucked away in the darkest part.

"Elan, don't leave me," she sighed as he kissed her neck.

"Never," the boy replied.

Wendell gave a small smile at their hidden affection and glanced at Jacques, thinking of the promises they had made to each other. He knew he would stay with Jacques for the rest of time; their lives were intertwined now: the one who could not die, and the one who brought death. Together they could defy the fates bestowed upon them, and maybe even carve out new paths for the future.